WITCH ON A MISSION

A BLAIR WILKES MYSTERY

ELLE ADAMS

"No, we don't currently have any clients looking for aspiring opera singers."

I put down the phone, shaking my head. Weird calls were par for the course in our line of work, but an opera-singing goblin was a new one. Just another day in the office of Eldritch & Co.

Bethan, my colleague and the boss's daughter, raised an eyebrow at me. "Opera singer?"

"Do you, by any chance, have any clients who might be looking for a goblin who can hit high notes?" I asked.

"No," she said. "That's a new one."

"I said we'd keep an eye out. Or should I have said 'ear' out?" I reached out to steady the small mountain of papers on Bethan's desk before they scattered all over the floor. The brunette witch had the magical gift of multitasking, which meant working beside her felt like sitting next to a highly efficient human hurricane. In addition to the piles on her desk, yet more papers overflowed from the drawer beneath, which I'd long suspected of having more dimensions than one would normally expect.

Rob, our werewolf co-worker, looked up. "I've no idea about opera singers, but the pack's band is looking for a new drummer."

"I thought it was for werewolves only." I raised a brow. "Besides, do you really want to subject any of our clients to the pack's singing?"

Nobody should voluntarily have to listen to the werewolf band's mangled attempts at music, and even most shifters knew to avoid the New Moon pub during one of their infamous free concerts.

He grinned. "You never know. Some people find the sound of wailing cats and crashing drums therapeutic."

Beside him, Lizzie, the fourth member of our team, looked up from typing. "Sounds like most werewolves do."

"Most of us have too much pent-up angst." Rob, who looked like he'd never suffered a minute of angst in his life, returned to his paperwork. "All the wailing and crashing is supposed to be symbolic."

"It's the cymbals that are the problem," said Bethan. "And the rest of it. My coven tried to host a meeting in the pub next door to the New Moon and we had to resort to communicating by passing notes around because none of us could hear a word the others said."

The printer—one of Lizzie's own creations—chose that moment to burst into a loud rendition of *O Come All Ye Faithful*. Lizzie, on a mission to get the office into the holiday spirit, had reprogrammed it the other week, with the result that all our paperwork now printed on

Christmas cards and the clients we interviewed had to put up with a backdrop of loud carol-singing.

With tinsel around her neck and her braided hair embellished with sparkly decorations, Lizzie had embraced the holiday spirit more than the rest of us put together—with the exception of Veronica, whose office currently resembled Santa's grotto, complete with a pack of elves grinning from the corners. I didn't *think* they were real elves, just an enchantment. I expected they would have quit in protest at the indignity by now if they were real.

Dritch & Co might be a crowded and chaotic work environment, yet it had become as familiar to me as my home, and I was quite looking forward to my first Christmas in the office. Even if half our clients seemed to have made it their mission to drive us all mad before the year was out.

"I don't think we've ever had a singing goblin in here before," Lizzie said after the printer had finished its song. *"You should have invited him here for the novelty value, Blair."*

"I would if we didn't have enough to deal with." In the short time since I'd started work at Dritch & Co, we'd handled werewolves pretending to be wizards, a recent haunting, a dead body in the boss's office, and more paranormal shenanigans than the average recruitment company encountered in a lifetime. Which seemed appropriate, given that we *were* the only paranormal recruitment service that I knew of in existence. And definitely the only one with a singing printer which had once got into a fight with the town's gargoyle police force.

As I turned back to my client list, Veronica Eldritch walked in. Like her daughter, she was tall, pale and lean.

Her white hair hung past her shoulders, and despite the long tinsel scarf wrapped around her neck and the sparkly heels, she also wore an unusually sombre expression.

I'd worked here for almost six months, so by now, I knew something was wrong. Veronica didn't usually walk into the office: she bounded, sailed, or strode, depending on her mood. She didn't *walk*.

"We have targets," she announced.

"Targets?" I said.

"Yes, Blair, targets," she said. "Why haven't you finished your list yet?"

"The last client was a goblin who was only interested in singing opera," I explained. "I said I'd wait and see if anything suitable shows up."

"There is no time for waiting," said Veronica. "The holidays are almost upon us, and we must reach the end of the list before the new year. Next time, hang up."

"What's the rush?" Bethan asked her mother. "Unless you have a cloning spell, there's no way we'll get through the whole list by the holidays. Just handling the people who want to hire a group of elves to sing carols or a pixie to volunteer to balance on top of their tree is taking up ninety percent of our time."

"Not to mention the wizard who wanted a herd of unicorns instead of reindeer," I added. "Anyway, I thought we were ahead of schedule."

"We are, but the list just keeps getting longer." Veronica added another stack of papers to the ones on her daughter's desk, nudging my own stack aside. "Deal with the time-sensitive ones first, won't you?"

She backed out of the office, trailing tinsel everywhere.

"Who's putting pressure on us?" I whispered. "I thought we were handling the increase in business pretty well, considering how many people want the elves to join their choir. No wonder they hide in the forest at this time of year."

"I wonder if someone's bothering her?" said Bethan. "She knows there's only four of us and a hundred clients with unreasonable demands. We'll be lucky to get through half of this before Christmas."

"No time like the present." I turned to the next client on my list, seeing a familiar name.

Erin Harker... my boyfriend Nathan's sister.

I stared at her name for a moment. Nathan's younger sister was the only one of his family members I'd met so far who hadn't hated me on sight, but that didn't change the fact that she was an ex-paranormal hunter, and to say the rest of her family didn't like me was an understatement. Her dad reportedly wasn't pleased with his daughter for leaving the hunters in order to go job-hunting in the paranormal world, and the last thing I needed was *him* calling the office when he found out she'd tried to hire me to find her a job here in Fairy Falls.

It might not be that big a deal. Maybe she wants to join the security team like her brother. Erin had renounced the hunters, and I doubted she was playing a joke on me. For all I knew, she'd be easier to handle than our other clients of the day.

I dialled her number, and someone picked up right away. "Hello, this is Dritch & Co recruitment—"

"Oh, hey, Blair!" Erin said brightly.

"Hey, Erin," I said. "You wanted to hire us?"

"Of course I do," she said. "I understand why my brother never wanted to leave Fairy Falls. I'd have happily stayed another week. I've told everyone all about the drunk elf, the pixie—and your cat, of course."

I gripped the phone. "You told everyone? Like who?"

The incident in question—my first meeting with Nathan's family—was one I'd have been happy to erase from my memory altogether, if not for the well-documented downsides of memory charms. The evening my cat had crashed my boyfriend's dinner party along with a pixie and a troop of elves was ranked at the very top of the most humiliating experiences in my lifetime, and I'd rather sing carols in an elf costume at the academy's Christmas pantomime than relive it.

"Joking, joking," said Erin. "I know, I'm not allowed to tell normals anything about our world. I've been good, honest. So… is anyone in town looking to hire an ex-hunter?"

"Are you sure?" I couldn't help asking. "If your dad or brothers find out—"

"They don't own me," she said. "I want to hire you."

"You mean, you want to hire Eldritch & Co," I said. "Look, I'd love to help you, but ninety percent of our clients are looking specifically for witches or wizards to work for them. Or carol-singing elves and unicorns who can pretend to be reindeer."

I'd never placed an ex-hunter before, but we weren't exactly swimming in applications from people who'd once made a living from hunting down magical criminals. Paranormal hunters rarely left the field, and most found it hard to fit in among paranormals due to their reputation for arresting anyone who they perceived to be flaunting the laws. As head of the town's security team, Nathan was an exception, but he wasn't the sort who got a kick out of abusing his power.

"I like a challenge," said Erin. "I'm staying at a hotel in town, by the way. Nobody's going to come along and haul me back to join the hunters. I've washed my hands of them."

Bethan nudged me in the side and indicated the towering stack of papers, as though to remind me that we still had a small mountain of clients to get through.

Ii took in a deep breath. If I was going to be with Nathan for the long-term, I'd have to get used to dealing with his family, and so far, Erin *was* the only one of them who could stand to be around me, let alone the madcap town I'd come to love. I could do worse than try to find her a position in Fairy Falls. "Okay. If you'd like to discuss your options in person—"

"I can be there in half an hour."

All right. At the very least, I'd be able to tick her name off my list, and if she'd come alone, the hunters might not even know she was here.

"Okay," I said. "See you later."

I put the phone down, mentally crossing my fingers that I hadn't made a mistake.

"Who was it?" asked Lizzie. "Not one of your favourite clients, since you look like you just swallowed a jug of mandrake juice."

"It was Erin. Nathan's sister."

"Isn't she a hunter?" Rob looked up, his brow furrowing.

"If she's looking for a new job, I guess not," said Bethan.

"She quit the hunters a couple of months ago," I explained. "Guess she felt more at home in the paranormal world. She liked Fairy Falls when she was visiting, so she's back in town looking for employment."

"I'd better warn my cousin," said Rob, rising to his feet.

"Would she have a problem?" Callie, our receptionist, didn't seem to mind Nathan, despite being the daughter of the grumpy werewolf chief who distrusted all hunters on principle. Callie was the chief's exact opposite personality-wise and Rob was even more easy-going, so his reaction took me by surprise.

"Not usually," he said. "Just wanted to make sure she knows."

The blond werewolf slipped out of the room, and I heard him and Callie conversing in low voices.

"Is there something going on that I don't know about?" I asked the others.

"Your guess is as good as mine," said Bethan.

"I thought the wolves were cool with us." Lizzie glanced up from typing. "Since you've helped half the chief's relatives find employment by now."

"Hey, Callie was already here." In fact, it had been Callie who'd called me offering employment here at Dritch & Co back when I'd thought I was normal. As there was a notable shortage of employment opportunities in the middle of the forest, more and more shifters had been coming to us for help with finding a job, so I'd assumed the werewolf chief's long-standing dislike of Dritch & Co had taken a back seat.

"True," said Bethan. "Still, you know how they feel about the hunters."

Werewolves typically regarded outsiders as suspicious, none more so than the paranormal hunters. After all, they had a not-unfounded reputation for being the shoot-first-and-ask-questions-later type who particularly disliked shifters, and personally, I thought the werewolves had good reason to be paranoid. The hunters had given my dad a lifelong jail sentence, after all, while my mother had died while on the run from them—and to complicate matters, it had been Mr Harker who'd heard my mum's last words. Nathan knew that, but not Erin.

Let's just say I was glad I wouldn't be spending the holidays with Nathan's family. I wasn't yet sure what I'd be doing over Christmas and the new year, for that matter, since my foster parents were currently in Australia and had no idea the paranormal world existed—let alone that I was a witch, dating a hunter, and neck-deep in requests for carol-singing elves. Who in their right mind would believe it if they hadn't lived it?

I tugged out Erin's CV from the towering stack of files and turned to the next candidate. "This guy wants to hire a yeti to tow his sleigh."

"Tell him they're all at the north pole at this time of year," said Bethan. "If you ask me, we should just tell the time-wasters that we've closed early for the holidays."

Rob re-entered the office, his usual smile absent. Before I could ask what was wrong, there came the sound of the front door sliding open. *There's Erin.*

I walked into the reception area as Nathan's sister walked in. As usual, she was dressed more like she was on her way to a hike than an interview, with mud around the hems of her trousers and on her thick boots.

"Blair!" She bounded over and hugged me. "Great to see you again. I'm sure you have a lot of new gossip on the ridiculous things my brother has done lately, haven't you?"

"Uh, we can catch up later," I said. "We're kind of swamped in end-of-year clients right now. But if you're in town for a while—"

"Oh, I'm staying here for a few weeks," she said. "We can catch up at the pub later. I liked that one—the Troll's Tavern, isn't it?"

It sounded like she'd come here alone. As long as the rest of her family stayed away, maybe this wouldn't be too bad.

"Blair, are you coming to do the interview?" Bethan called from behind the door to our office.

"Yes, of course. This way, Erin." I led the way into our cosy office, where she stopped to admire the bedecked Christmas tree in the corner and the tinsel-covered coffee machine, which had added several festive options to its menu courtesy of Lizzie. The small interview room was one of the few places in the office which remained more or less the same as it had before.

"You really are getting into the spirit of the season." Erin perched on the edge of the interview chair. "Speaking of spirits, I heard you had a ghost in here on Samhain."

"Half the town was infested with them." I sat in the other chair and studied her CV. "It says here you worked for a furniture company for the last month. Was that in the normal world?"

She looked more like she'd feel at home destroying furniture with an axe rather than selling it.

"I did," she said. "But after experiencing the paranormal world, it's hard to leave it behind, you know? I often wonder what type of magic I'd have if I was a witch."

"You have the ability to see through illusions like Nathan, right?" I scanned her CV. "That might come in handy. I'm sure we can find you a position, but we might have to wait until after the holidays. Most seasonal positions are filled by now."

She leaned forward. "Take your time. I guess you don't get a lot of ex-hunter clients?"

"You're my first," I admitted. "Like I said—I mostly work with witches and wizards. But I've helped other paranormals who can't use magic to find a suitable position for their needs."

The trouble was, even jobs that didn't require actual magic use often required all employees to carry a wand and have magic-based qualifications. Furthermore, being an ex-hunter meant she'd be treated with extra scrutiny than most. But Nathan had made it work. I could always ask him for advice on how he'd handled the process when he'd left the hunters.

She fidgeted in her seat. "I'm not sure I'm cut out for a desk job."

"Is there a particular area you're interested in?" I asked.

"Lots of things," she said. "I was looking into detective work. I have experience in that area, just… not with the regular police."

Hmm. "Do your brothers and father know you're here?"

"No," she said. "I mean, they might, but it's been months since I moved away. They assumed I'd never make anything of myself without the hunters. I tried fitting in with the normals, but it didn't work, so here I am."

I knew what it felt like to not quite belong in either the paranormal or normal world. I also had zero contacts with any law enforcement… except, that is, for the gargoyles who currently ran the town's police force. To say Steve wasn't my biggest fan was like saying the north pole was a bit chilly, but technically, Nathan was in charge of the town's security team despite being below Steve on the ladder. Maybe it'd count as cheating for him to hire his own sister, but it was worth a try.

"I'll give the police a call and see if they have any positions open," I told her.

Her eyes brightened. "Thanks, Blair. You're amazing."

"I'll let you know by the end of the week." I got to my feet. "It might be after the holidays, mind, but I'll do my best."

As she left, the printer broke into a loud rendition of *Rudolph the Red-Nosed Reindeer* and spat a wad of green-and-red paper after her.

"Sorry, our office printer is a little overactive," I told her, picking up the paper. "I think it's given you a Christmas card."

"Neat," she said, taking the card from me. "I've never got a card from a magical printer before. I'll frame it and hang it on the wall."

Absolutely nothing seemed to bother Erin. Small wonder when her previous career had involved chasing down paranormal criminals. She could certainly handle herself—I just hoped the rest of the town could handle her.

Rob watched Erin leave the office, but he didn't offer a comment. Given werewolves' enhanced hearing, he'd probably heard at least some of our interview, but I didn't see why the chief of the werewolves would react any differently to her being here than any of the other people we'd hired from outside Fairy Falls.

If I called Steve and told him what Erin wanted, he'd laugh in my face. Or growl at me. Steve had no sense of humour to speak of, and the festive season seemed to have put him in an even worse mood than usual. It was all very well imagining sweet-talking the grumpiest gargoyle in town into hiring another ex-hunter, but to him, I was a nuisance at best, a danger at worst. No, it was Nathan I needed to speak to.

I called him as I was leaving work, and he picked up right away.

"Hey, Blair," he said. "Something up?"

"Why would there be?"

"If things were fine, you'd just text."

He had a point there. "Things *are* fine. I just had an unexpected new client today."

"My sister."

"You knew?"

"She texted me on her way into town."

"At least she told you," I said. "She wants to work for Steve. I don't suppose he's magically swapped personalities with someone nice lately?"

"No."

Figures.

"She also talked me into going with her to the pub later," I added. "You're invited, if you're off duty."

"I will be by the end of your magic lesson. I'll talk to Steve before I leave and let him know Erin's interested in a position working for our security team."

"You're a lifesaver," I said. "Really."

"Anything to help you avoid seeing Steve any more than you have to," he said mildly. "See you later, Blair."

His voice made me feel warm and happy inside, and nothing cheered me more than the prospect of an extra date with him, even with his sister there. That he'd taken Steve off my hands was more than welcome, too. Now all I needed was to get through today's magic lesson. Despite the lingering worry of what the hunters might say if they found out another Harker sibling had moved to Fairy Falls, I felt pretty pleased with myself.

2

The classroom in which I took my magic classes with Rita was one of few places in town which hadn't been decorated with a towering Christmas tree. After all, anything inside the room was liable to end up being levitated, dyed, or transformed into household objects, depending on the day's lessons.

Rita, my tutor, was a tall forty-something witch with curly dyed red hair and arms adorned with bangles. She watched as my fellow apprentice witch, Rebecca, raised the sceptre into the air. The giant carved stick looked almost too heavy for her to lift, and Rebecca needed both hands to point it at the piece of paper she was meant to be levitating. The sceptre's purple gem gleamed with violet light and the piece of paper on the desk gave a feeble flop.

"Hang on," said Rebecca. "I've got it…"

Another wave, and the paper flopped off the desk and onto the carpet like a dead fish.

"Better than the last time," said Rita.

Rebecca hung her head. "That's not saying much. Last time it didn't even move."

"You need more of a sweeping motion." Rita used her wand to demonstrate. The paper hopped back onto the desk in a swift, precise movement. I'd seen Rebecca pull off the spell with no issues using her wand, but the sceptre was too cumbersome for her to manoeuvre without both hands, which threw off her aim. Being chosen as the region's new Head Witch was taking her some adjustment, especially as an eleven-year-old who'd only been learning magic for a few months.

According to tradition, the sceptre's wielder had to carry it around with them everywhere for the year they wielded it—which for Rebecca, meant taking it to school. Rebecca was self-conscious enough about being behind her classmates on magic without adding the pressure of being the youngest Head Witch in history on top of it. I didn't blame her classmates for being overly curious, considering it was unheard of for the sceptre to wind up in the hands of an underage witch. Even Madame Grey didn't fully understand how it'd happened. As her fellow apprentice witch, I took evening lessons alongside her and had persuaded Rita to use our allotted hour to help Rebecca learn to cast basic spells using the sceptre rather than doing so during school hours.

Her fluffy cat familiar, Toast, mewed in encouragement as Rebecca raised the sceptre once again. This time, a blast of wind swept through the room, rattling the desks and causing Rita's bangles to jingle. The paper flew into the air, and Rebecca let out a cry of triumph. Then the desk flew up to join it, followed by a chair.

"Uh-oh." Rebecca fought to bring the sceptre under

control, but it was too late. One piece of furniture after another left the ground, caught in the whirling dervish of her spell. To my alarm, I found my feet leaving the ground, too, and Toast gave a piteous yowl as he floated past.

"Rebecca!" said Rita. "Calm yourself."

Rebecca's hands trembled on the sceptre, and the floating objects began to spin in tighter circles. "I can't!"

I caught my balance in mid-air, glad I'd spent so many hours trying to master the use of Seven Millimetre Boots and my fairy wings.

"Yes, you can," I said. "Just wave the sceptre in the reverse movement. You've done it with a wand a dozen times."

Mouth trembling, Rebecca waved the sceptre, using both arms to keep it steady.

Everything stopped spinning. Toast landed on the bookshelf with a distressed meow. I, meanwhile, did a pirouette and landed on the floor in a feat of athleticism I'd probably never repeat again. I sank into an accidental bow and caught my balance on the edge of the nearest desk.

Rita waved her wand, and in a flash of light, everything in the room returned to its former place. "There."

Rebecca lowered the sceptre, her eyes brimming with tears. "I'm sorry. I don't know what happened. I just can't control it."

"You can use its magic and you can control it... just not at the same time," said Rita.

"Yet," I added.

Rita nodded to me. "Blair knows a thing or two about applying moderation."

That was a nice way of saying my control over my magic went out the window when I was under stress. "Once you've got the hang of it, you'll be amazing. Trust me."

Rebecca shook her head. "The sceptre is stronger than I am. Maybe I have to wait until I'm older to be able to control it. Or maybe I'm too late, because I started magic lessons years after I was supposed to."

"Age has nothing to do with magical talent," Rita says firmly. "Experience engenders knowledge and wisdom, yes, but you can still learn to use the sceptre for any spell you can use a wand for. In the meantime, Madame Grey and I will impart our own knowledge and wisdom."

"But that sounds like I'll have the sceptre for years." Rebecca looked at her in horror. "It can't choose me as Head Witch again, right? I thought it was a fluke. Someone else should be chosen next time."

"We cannot guarantee that," said Rita. "Therefore, we have to proceed ahead as we always do when a new wielder is chosen. It's our duty to prepare you, Rebecca."

"For what?" Rebecca said tremulously. "Everyone laughing at me and not taking me seriously? Or trying to steal it? The last bearer was over seventy years older than me and someone even managed to steal it from her." Her hands clenched at her sides, her breaths coming quickly.

My heart ached for her. I'd caused an endless number of magical accidents since my arrival in Fairy Falls, but I'd had more time than Rebecca had to get used to being under the spotlight, and she was at an age where she was desperate to fit in with her classmates. More to the point, the sceptre *had* gone missing under my roof, and people had been murdered for it. Who could blame Rebecca for being freaked out at the concept of being its wielder for an indefinite amount of time?

"You'll get there," I told her. "Don't worry."

Why did people say that, anyway? Especially when there usually *was* something to worry about. I didn't know what I'd have done in her position, but with both Rita and Madame Grey tutoring her, she was just going to have to try her best. The sceptre had chosen her for a reason, and her lack of confidence wouldn't always be a barrier.

"I think that's it for today," said Rita. "Rebecca, go to see Madame Grey for a progress update, okay?"

Rebecca left the room with her head down, while Rita beckoned to me to stay behind. *Was I supposed to stop her from levitating the whole room?* I couldn't even keep my own magic under control most of the time, let alone someone else's.

My tutor's brow was wrinkled in concern. "I won't be able to put off her first visit to the other witch communities forever. After the new year, she'll have to start performing her public role, provided it fits in with her classes."

"She's right, though—there are people who might try to steal the sceptre from her," I pointed out. "I know the Rosemary witches are in jail, but a child claiming the sceptre is big news in the magical world. Covens all over Lancashire are talking about her."

I knew, because they kept calling up Dritch & Co to tell me so.

"I'm aware of that, Blair," she said. "I'm confident that Rebecca's gift will help her deter any potential thieves, but

I've asked that nobody share any details of her talent with anyone from outside the town."

"Wouldn't they be more likely to target her if they didn't know she can alter their personalities just by making eye contact?"

"Not necessarily," said Rita. "She isn't without protection, either. Someone is always watching both her and the sceptre."

"That probably isn't helping her nerves." She had a point about Rebecca's magical gift, though. She'd even used it on the former Head Witch… a story which, without context, was bound to make everyone think twice about challenging her.

I just wished I could do something to make Rebecca feel better about her unwanted new Head Witch title. It had been almost two months since Samhain, and if anything, her nerves had grown worse over time, not better.

"I know you're doing your best to help her, Blair," said Rita. "You may leave."

I walked out of the classroom, then did a double-take as I spotted a pale brunette lurking in the lobby. Blythe Dailey—Rebecca's older sister, my ex-co-worker, and the person who'd given me no end of grief since I'd moved to Fairy Falls. No wonder Rebecca had been so nervous today. Blythe had been studiously avoiding me since her sister's magical gift had compelled her to ask for my help and her mother had ended up in jail for trying to use Rebecca's talents to bring down Madame Grey and the leading witch covens, but she must know her sister and I took classes together. What was she doing here?

"Hey, Blair," she said. "Nice dance."

My cheeks heated. Of course she'd been peeking through the door when I'd performed that awkward landing after Rebecca's levitating spell.

"Thanks," I said. "Did you just come here to compliment me or is there something you wanted to ask me?"

She gave a short, humourless laugh. "You were helping my sister."

"Well observed."

"And it's not going well."

I raised an eyebrow. "Aren't you supposed to be supportive of your younger sibling? I'd have thought you'd be proud of her."

Blythe paused for a long moment. "She shouldn't have been chosen as Head Witch."

"Bit late for that," I said. "Anyway, it's not my decision to make."

"No, but you can talk to Madame Grey and the others," she insisted. "The local coven leaders will listen to you."

"I can't ask everyone to defy a tradition that existed decades before I moved here," I pointed out.

"You're a force of destruction, Blair," she said. "If anyone can do it, you can."

I blinked. "You have a really weird way of paying compliments."

"It wasn't a compliment."

Figures. "I'm trying to help your sister, Blythe, but I can't do the impossible. Rita was pretty clear that she has to learn how to use magic with the sceptre. Once she gets the hang of it, people will know to stay out of her way."

Her hands clenched at her sides. "It won't work. People will challenge her no matter what, and I'd rather see her have to give it up than see her taken advantage of."

"By who?" I said. "Your mother?"

My mother had once tried to steal the sceptre, according to the former Head Witch. Did Blythe and her mum know? It wouldn't surprise me, given their history. At least Blythe didn't seem to share her mother's ambitions. I didn't know how frequently she and Rebecca interacted now they no longer lived in the same house, but it wasn't hard to guess that Mrs Dailey would be scheming if she'd heard about her daughter's unexpected elevation to Head Witch. It was bad enough that she'd unscrupulously tried to use Rebecca's magical gifts for her own gain, and I shuddered to think what she might have done with the sceptre if she hadn't been locked in jail for conspiring against Madame Grey.

"Everyone will want to take advantage," Blythe said. "Did you really expect all the covens in the region would let a kid be chosen as Head Witch without a fuss?"

"I thought it was a ceremonial title and nothing else," I said. "Rita keeps saying so, anyway."

"Not to others," she said. "Even outside the magical community."

"Outside? Normals don't know about us."

"Not *normals,* idiot."

Was she implying the *hunters* might take an interest in Rebecca's talent? Granted, Mrs Dailey had allied with the hunters herself—the same hunters, I now knew, who'd been the last people to see my mother alive.

But the hunters weren't magical. They couldn't use the sceptre, and it made no sense for them to have any interest in Rebecca. Blythe might be paranoid, but if I'd learned one thing from the time I'd spent in the magical world, it was not to get complacent.

After all, it was just over a week until the winter solstice, the second and only chance this year I'd have to talk to my father. If the hunters came back for any reason, that opportunity would evaporate into thin air. My dad had warned me to leave town after he'd learned of the hunters' interest in me, but I hadn't heard a word about the Inquisitor since his unexpected visit over the summer. *He* wouldn't have any reason to target Rebecca—right?

"Blythe, if you know something, tell me," I said. "If Rebecca is in danger, you have to tell Madame Grey or Rita at the very least."

"It's nothing," she said.

Lie. Obviously.

"I mean, nothing concrete," she added. "I don't know about a specific threat, and... why am I even bothering with you, Blair?"

She turned around to leave, and the front doors blew open. A few men ran into the lobby, all huge blond guys. Werewolves. Specifically, werewolves from the family who led the pack. Callie's cousin, a guy who looked so much like Rob that he must be his brother, stopped in the middle of the carpeted lobby, beside the towering Christmas tree.

"Alec is dead," he said. "He was shot on our own territory."

I backed up from the group of bristling werewolves. "Shot by who?"

"Your boyfriend Nathan was there," said a rangy man with a mop of straw-like hair. "Patrolling the border when Alec died. What have you to say to that, Blair Wilkes?"

3

"Nathan?" I said. "He's been patrolling the border for years. It's his job. Did he see what happened?"

"No," said a younger werewolf with close-cropped blond hair. "But we found him less than a mile from the site where the body was found, and he wasn't scheduled to be patrolling there today. He had no good reason to be there."

"He often goes walking in the forest," I said. "I didn't know you knew his schedule, besides."

"I don't." He snapped his mouth shut. "I said it wrong, didn't I?"

Callie's cousin scowled. "Stop talking, Julius."

I frowned at him. "Did you ask him to accuse Nathan?"

"Who else carries a gun containing silver bullets?" he responded, his lip curling.

The chief had never liked that Nathan was allowed to wander in and out of the forest at will. Back when he'd been a paranormal hunter, Nathan had been forced to apprehend a rogue wolf from a different local pack and the chief had never quite forgiven him for it. He was still friendly with some of the other shifters, but werewolves could hold a grudge like nobody else. That was no reason to accuse Nathan of committing murder, though.

Before anyone could say another word, the door slammed open again and Rob ran into the entrance hall.

"Blair can set this straight," he said, breathless, addressing his brother. "She can tell truth from lie, Claude."

"Aren't the police there?" Over my dead body would I set one foot in the forest with the wolves on full alert after a murder.

"They're on their way," said Claude. "Gargoyles find it hard to fly deep in the forest."

I'll bet. "And Nathan? He's not still in the forest, is he?"

"If you want to see him," Callie's cousin said, "you'd better come with us, Blair."

"I thought you wanted her to do the questioning," said Rob.

"Hang on. Don't I get a say in this?" Every attempt I'd ever made to reason with the werewolf chief had ended in disaster. Our last encounter had been positively mellow, but a werewolf shot dead on his own territory would have sparked the chief's infamous hair-trigger temper. At the best of times, trying to have a friendly chat with a guy who could transform into a giant furry wolf when he got mad was like prodding a sleeping chimera in the rear with a sharp instrument.

Not that I was keen on the idea of leaving Nathan to the literal wolves, either. As for the police, Steve made no secret of his annoyance that Nathan's security team had overtaken his fellow gargoyles in terms of efficiency. I wouldn't put it past him to use the situation to his advantage.

Great. I guess that means I'm going to run with the wolves. I just hoped the night wouldn't end with me running *from* the wolves.

"I'll come, but only if you promise neither Nathan nor I will be arrested," I said. "And that nobody will retaliate if I use my lie-sensing ability to question anyone you ask me to."

"They won't," said Rob, with a pointed glance at Claude. "I'll make sure of it. We need this dealt with before the chief makes a rash decision."

"Rash decisions?" Claude said. "You're hiring a human? Or whatever she is?"

"Hey!" I protested. "I'm not getting paid for this, you know. If you want to rely on Steve, feel free to ask him to step in, but we're talking about the guy who'd arrest a tree if it looked at him the wrong way."

"She's right," piped up Julius.

"Shut it," snapped Claude. "Fine. Come with us, but only if you behave yourself."

You can talk. Knowing werewolves, the quicker the real culprit was caught, the better. They'd almost gone to war with the local vampires over the summer after suspecting them of a different crime, and their relationship with the paranormal hunters was even more contentious. After all, most hunters had apprehended at least one rogue were-wolf for attacking a human.

I looked around for Blythe, but she'd slipped away halfway through our conversation. No surprises there.

For now, Blythe, Rebecca and the sceptre would have to wait.

I had to help Nathan.

———

The werewolves' territory covered the north side of the forest. They usually didn't let any trespassers cross the invisible dividing line between their part of the woods and everywhere else, but the town's security team was supposed to be an exception. Nobody had ever challenged Nathan before, but then again, nobody had ever been shot at the town's border either. If another rule-flaunting hunter like Sleepy, Dopey or Grumpy had gone rogue and let Nathan take the blame, I'd make sure they ended up behind bars this time.

The forest path wound between oak and ash trees, a web of branches forming a canopy above our heads. While the other werewolves walked ahead, Rob hung back to keep pace with me.

"Sorry for dragging you into this, Blair," he said. "Truthfully, I don't just need you to question the suspects. The weapon that killed Alec is nowhere to be found, and while Nathan is unarmed, the fact that he was found at the murder scene seems too suspicious for the others to let go."

My heart lurched. "What—you think someone set him up on purpose?"

"Maybe. It's the worst-case scenario." Droplets of rainwater fell from an overhead branch and he shook his head to dislodge them.

"Who'd want to frame Nathan?" I whispered. "I can't

see any of the hunters turning on him. Unless Sleepy, Dopey and Grumpy are back."

"Who?"

"Mrs Dailey's allies," I said. "They got fired for their role in her plan, but they're still walking free and might have access to their weapons."

Rob's expression darkened. "I hope you're wrong."

Nathan was innocent, but Erin's appearance in town right before the murder didn't help matters. I hoped the werewolves didn't know about her—aside from Rob and Callie, that is. *What awful timing.*

We took a shortcut through some undergrowth which tangled around my ankles. Pulling my coat free from the brambles, I jumped when a shrill voice swore loudly. "Tread on my tail, why don't you?"

"Is someone in there?" I called.

A head popped up from the brambles with long whiskers and wispy brown hair. "Yes, there is."

"Sorry. Didn't see you."

The man looked up at me through watery blue eyes. "I get that a lot. Do you know what those werewolves are yelling about?"

The werewolves in question turned back to look at him. "Who are you?" asked Rob.

"I'm a rat shifter. Name's Anton. What's all that racket about?"

"A werewolf died," said Rob. "Murdered, in fact. I'd advise you to steer clear of the werewolves' territory until we figure out what happened."

"Murdered?" His eyes widened. "I'm terribly sorry."

Lie. From what I'd heard, the other shifters and the werewolves did not get along one bit.

A howl sounded from deeper in the woods, and the rat shifter paled. Then he darted back into the undergrowth in a flash, shifting into rat form. I glimpsed a long tail disappear behind him and found myself envying his ability to make a quick getaway. The last thing I wanted to do was walk *towards* the sound of the horrible howling, but Nathan's freedom might depend on it. Besides, I trusted Rob to make sure Nathan and I wouldn't get torn apart by wolves. *I hope.*

"Don't worry," Rob whispered to me. "That's Alec's family, mourning their eldest son. They aren't the ones who found Nathan or the body."

We came to a halt in a clearing full of blond werewolves, including the pack beta, Bryan, who glared in my direction when Rob and I approached. I assumed an expression I hoped looked suitably sombre while bracing myself to transform into my fairy form and fly away if they turned on me. Nathan was nowhere in sight. *It can't be a trap, can it? Rob wouldn't do that to me.*

Chief Donovan stepped forward. Huge and blond like the rest of his family, he studied me with narrowed eyes. "Blair Wilkes. I would like you to find out what happened to Alec."

"You want…" I trailed off. "You *asked* Rob to bring me here?"

No wonder they hadn't chased me off, despite Claude's disapproval. Not that they exactly looked thrilled to see me, mind, but I'd never have expected the chief of the werewolf pack to *want* me involved with the murder investigation.

"What else?" He indicated another blond werewolf

who might have been Rob's brother or cousin. "Gregor found the body."

"I did," confirmed Gregor.

True.

The chief looked expectantly at me. "Well?"

Wait, did he want me to use my lie-sensing power? "Um, he's telling the truth."

The chief nodded. Since when did he even believe my lie-sensing power actually worked, let alone trust me to use it to question his fellow werewolves? Did he not trust his own people? In fact, did he think one of *them* might be the killer?

"Do you know how he died?" I asked, taking the chief's silence as an indication to proceed with the questioning.

"He appeared to have been shot," said Gregor. "When we examined the wound, we found a type of silver bullet that only the paranormal hunters are known to use. After thoroughly inspecting the crime scene, we allowed Alec's family to take their son's body for the mourning ceremony. We found no other traces of the weapon or the murderer at the scene of his death."

My lie-sensing ability remained quiet, so it seemed he spoke the truth.

"Where is Nathan, then?" I asked.

"I left some of the pack members watching over him," said Claude. "One of the people who found him is Alec's cousin, so he has good reason to hate the hunters."

"Alec's family is related to the pack your hunter friend had an unfortunate relationship with," explained the chief.

My heart sank. Nathan had apprehended a rogue member of another pack, and I hadn't known any relations or friends of that werewolf were among the chief's people.

"Were there any witnesses?" I asked.

Claude bared his teeth. "Are you calling me a liar?"

"No, but I have to ask questions if I want to get to the bottom of this," I said calmly. "Your uncle asked me to investigate."

His nostrils flared. "No witnesses, but nobody except the hunters uses those bullets."

"Exactly," Julius chipped in. "That's why one of them must have done it."

"And you didn't find the murder weapon?" I turned to the chief, who gave Claude a disapproving look.

"No, we did not," he said.

"Nathan was unarmed when you caught him," I went on. "He doesn't carry a gun with silver bullets, anyway." I wouldn't have thought the chief would let him within ten miles of the pack if he still had any of his old hunter weapons, even if he didn't actually use them.

"Alec was found alone near the town's north border," said the chief. "I have no doubt there are a number of hunters who would find it an amusing sport to take shots at us from a distance, but Nathan wouldn't be that stupid. He *works* at the police station, and knows he'd be the first person we'd suspect."

Except for Erin. But if the others didn't know she was in town, I wasn't about to enlighten them. Besides, she was applying for jobs, not wandering around the forest.

"You've grown soft," Claude told the pack chief. "If we start making friends with those hunters, they'll flock to town and set up shop here."

"Nathan isn't a hunter," I said, but a number of growls

drowned out my words, aimed at Claude. The werewolves agreed with the chief… that Nathan *wasn't* the killer?

"If you agree with my nephew, feel free to throw your lot in with him," growled the pack chief. "I, on the other hand, intend to find the real culprit. Blair, ask them if they saw anything."

"Uh." I looked around at the werewolves, wishing I'd rehearsed my questions. I hadn't expected to be asked to speak to so many of them at once. "Did any of you see the killer or the murder weapon?"

A chorus of 'no's followed. The chief turned back to me, an expectant look on his face.

"You want me to ask the whole pack?" I said. "Uh, if he was shot from the other side of the border, the perpetrator might have fled on foot. There are a lot of places to hide out there in the middle of nowhere. Why not let Nathan send a team out to search?"

"Two of Alec's friends insisted on watching over him." He pointed to another clearing visible through the trees. "We will handle his questioning now."

I followed Rob to where Nathan stood with his back to a large oak tree, a wolf on either side of him. Unlike the others, they were in wolf form and not human, their grey fur bristling, their eyes bright and angry. Nathan's expression was surprisingly calm for someone who was surrounded by a group of furious werewolves, at least until he saw me. Then, his eyes widened. "Blair, what are you doing here?"

"Hi." I glanced at the two wolves, then back at Nathan. "I'm supposed to question you next."

"Of course you'd defend him," said Claude's voice from behind me. "Uncle, if you wanted to hire a human to do the questioning, you might have picked someone who doesn't have a personal relationship with the accused."

"Blair is the only person in town who can tell truth from lie," Rob said. "Come on, shift into human form, you two. Blair can't understand your growling."

The two wolves shifted into human form… completely naked. One was blond, one dark-haired, and both just as hairy in human form as they were as wolves. I had no idea where to put my eyes, so I settled for watching Nathan instead. He didn't look hurt or even afraid, but he must be thinking hard about how to get out of this without anyone getting hurt.

"You're wasting your time hunting for another culprit when we have the killer right here," said the dark-haired werewolf on the left, making no move to cover himself. "This hunter once made a career out of treating our people like animals. Murder is nothing to him."

"I told you," Nathan said, "I'm not carrying a weapon. I can't possibly have shot anyone even if I had reason to, which I didn't. Any other hunter might have been on the other side of the border. I would be more than happy to lead a team to search the forest for any weapons they may have dropped—"

"Stay within my sight until I say otherwise," snapped the werewolf on the right. "As for you, Blair, this is a pack matter only."

"The chief told me to come here." *He didn't mention you wouldn't be wearing clothes, though.* Nathan didn't seem as embarrassed as I was, but then again, he'd probably seen all sorts while patrolling the forest on shifter territory. "Also, every word he just said is the truth. Nathan is innocent."

33

"Shame on you, chief," said the man on the left. "It's about time we returned to policing ourselves, not depending on these gargoyles and witches to keep our people safe. My cousin is dead, and I will have justice."

Nathan tensed, inching closer to me as the two werewolves advanced towards the chief and his blond contingent.

"What are you implying?" the chief said through bared teeth. "I am sorry for what happened to your cousin, but that is no excuse to provoke the hunters into retaliation. Let Nathan go."

Whoa. He was defending Nathan? If not for his furious expression, I might suspect he'd taken a dose of the potion the werewolves gave to their cubs to make them more docile during their first shift.

The two men advanced forward to speak to the chief, and as their voices rose in volume, Nathan moved closer to me.

"You shouldn't have come," he whispered.

"I wasn't about to leave you alone in here," I whispered back. "Besides, you're not the killer. Anyone who knows you will say the same."

"Yes, but it *was* a hunter's weapon that was used to commit the murder. Until an alternative shows up, I have to present myself for questioning by the police."

While most of the werewolves didn't seem to think he was guilty, it was Steve the gargoyle who had the power to pass judgement on him. And with no alternatives, Steve had a nasty habit of locking up the first vaguely guilty-looking person he found.

"Have you seen any other hunters near the town lately?" I asked in a low voice.

"My sister," he said. "But she wouldn't have brought any weapons here. She left every trace of her connection to the hunters behind when she quit."

"Does she know you're out here?" I asked. "I was supposed to be meeting her at the pub tonight."

"I know," he said. "I would guess that a hunter outsider was the killer, given the choice of weapon. For all our sakes, I hope the police come to the same conclusion."

Me too. I checked the werewolves weren't close enough to hear, then asked, "Nathan... has your father been near the border again?"

A long moment passed. "Recently? No. I can't see why he'd shoot a werewolf for no reason. He might be harsh, but he follows the law."

Mr Harker *made* the laws, or at least knew the people who did. Accusing *him* would be worse than throwing accusations at the pack chief.

The sound of beating wings came from above the canopy, which rustled as three gargoyles flew down to land in the clearing. Their huge leathery forms transformed into humans—thankfully, fully clothed ones. In the lead was Steve, who looked almost as gargoyle-like in his human form as he did as a leathery-winged snarling monster.

"Why am I not surprised to see you here, Blair Wilkes?" he said.

"Hey," I protested. "I was invited here, actually."

Steve made a disparaging noise. He knew all about my contentious relationship with the werewolf pack, not to mention my habit of showing up at murder scenes, but I wasn't the person who'd found the body this time.

The werewolves crowded around Steve and his two buddies.

"Alec is dead," Claude said. "He was shot with a hunter's weapon, and a silver bullet killed him outright. A cowardly killing."

Steve eyed Nathan. "What were you doing here, then? Just passing through?"

"Patrolling," he said. "I wasn't on the pack's territory at the time, and I'm unarmed."

"He might have thrown the murder weapon away to cover up his crime," said the younger werewolf, Julius.

"Search the area," Steve ordered his companions. As they took flight, he turned back to the werewolves. "Have any more outsiders been sighted in the area?"

More? Was he seriously implying that he thought Nathan was an outsider? He'd lived here for years. Anger brewed inside me and I found my fists clenching at my sides.

"No," said the chief, "but Alec was wandering alone near the border when he was shot."

"If you're suggesting it's his own fault he was shot by a foul silver weapon—" Claude said heatedly.

"I am not," said Chief Donovan. "Calm yourself, nephew. Justice will be served when we find the culprit."

Steve looked between them. "Unless you can confirm a pack member had access to the murder weapon, I will have to work with what I know."

Oh, man. That wasn't a good sign at all. Steve had worked with Nathan for years, but he also feared and distrusted the hunters more than most. Specifically, he feared they'd take his authority away. In the absence of

WITCH ON A MISSION

anyone else to blame, he might well throw his own ally under the bus. I didn't trust him an inch.

"It will take you all night to search the forest," said Nathan. "If there's a rogue hunter out there, the town's citizens need to be warned."

An uneasy silence fell over the gathering werewolves. If the culprit *was* a rogue hunter, and Steve kept it quiet and pinned the blame on Nathan instead, the murderer would be free to strike again. The gargoyle police chief was backed into a corner and he knew it. Then again, so were we.

"Feel free to warn them," said the chief. "Alec was shot, which suggests a human killer, but that might be what the murderer wanted us to assume."

"What shifter would use a hunter's gun to commit murder?" said Claude. "Enough of this. My uncle might not want to have you removed, hunter, but I will."

"I'm going to have to take you into custody," Steve told Nathan, in a rather pained voice as though he had a toothache.

"Excuse me?" said Nathan. "You have no proof of my guilt. I don't have a loaded gun anywhere in my possession, let alone any silver bullets. You're welcome to search my property if you don't believe me."

Steve scowled at him. "If you want to discuss the matter in more detail, you'll be spending the night in my office."

I started to protest, but Claude got there first. "He works next door to your office. That's no punishment."

"He's innocent!" I said. "You can't jail the head of your own security force, let alone someone who patrols the werewolves' territory on a regular basis because it's his job to keep everyone safe."

"Don't worry, Blair," Nathan said. "I'll be fine."

His words were about as reassuring as the 'don't worry' I'd given Rebecca earlier. While Nathan might work at the police office, the mere rumour of him being arrested would damage his reputation and might well cause others in town to jump to conclusions about his guilt.

"This is wrong," I whispered to Nathan, as Steve moved to converse with several of the werewolves.

He gave a reassuring squeeze of my shoulder. "This is the best way to avoid further conflict."

The best way to avoid a fight in the short term? Perhaps, but I had an inkling the matter wouldn't easily be brushed aside, least of all by the werewolves.

"Are you still here, Blair?" said Steve. "I'd suggest you go home."

I looked at Nathan, torn. "Should I talk to…"

Did the police even know Erin was in town?

"I'll handle everything," Nathan said. He wrapped me in a quick embrace which didn't last nearly long enough. "You should go home. I'll call my sister when I have time."

Good. The others don't know she's in town. After Nathan told her everything, she'd have more sense than to show up at my office again. Right?

4

An hour later, I'd finished updating Alissa, my flatmate, on the evening's unwelcome turn of events. Sky, my fluffy black cat familiar, curled up next to me on the sofa, purring.

"Cheer up, Blair," said Alissa. Her own familiar, Roald, occupied her lap.

"Little hard when I had to spend my night looking at naked werewolves and now my boyfriend's behind bars."

"He's not, is he?" she said, giving Roald a stroke. "Steve had to reassure the werewolves he was making an effort to solve the crime, I'll bet, but Nathan spends every other night at the police station anyway."

"Are you sure the whole town won't know he was a suspect by the week's end, though?" I said. "This is going to get the rumour mill spinning no matter what."

Alissa opened and closed her mouth. "Maybe the werewolves won't talk."

I made a sceptical noise. "They're more gossipy than the witches."

"True." She gave her familiar another stroke. "We know Nathan's innocent. Sounds like the chief does, too."

"Some of the other werewolves are looking for the first hunter to throw the blame at," I said. "And Steve's track record isn't exactly great."

"Not this time," said Alissa. "Nathan is head of the town's security team, and if another hunter is to blame, Steve will want to find them. Mark my words."

"I know he will." I had to trust Nathan would warn Erin, because I'd stupidly left her contact details at work with the other clients'. I'd never thought to ask him if *she* carried a weapon, but she was neither an active hunter nor a murderer. Still, if the gargoyles got so much as a whiff that she was in town, she'd be in danger of ending up in an interrogation room instead of an interview chair.

Sky yawned and stretched. "Miaow."

"See, He agrees with me," said Alissa.

Sky sounded more like he wanted me to stroke him, which I did. I wanted to believe the chief would keep his angry pack members in line and Steve would take the common sense approach, but knowing Nathan might take the fall for someone else's crime made worry fill my chest like a swarm of angry bees.

"So much for a date night," I said. "I mean, it wouldn't have been a proper date with Erin there anyway."

"I was going to ask if you wanted to come on a double date with Samuel and me," she said. "You know, when all this calms down."

"Assuming neither of ends up in jail?" I said. "Sure. Things are going well with Samuel, then?"

The vampire librarian's interest in Alissa had initially taken me by surprise, though maybe it shouldn't have.

Alissa freely admitted she had questionable taste in guys, as evidenced by her previous relationship with the werewolf pack's beta, as well as a newly turned vampire who'd also happened to be one of her patients at the hospital. But Samuel seemed a genuinely decent guy, for one of the living dead.

"Believe it or not, they are," she said. "He has this knack for guessing what I'm thinking at any given time."

"Mind-reading tends to give you that advantage."

She gave a sheepish grin. "He's very polite about it. Anyway, it's better than turning into a wolf at the full moon."

"As long as he doesn't bite you."

"Vampire bites don't turn you unless you also drink their blood," she reminded me. "Otherwise, they're quite relaxing."

"I didn't need to know that, Alissa."

"Miaow," said Sky, in tones that implied he agreed.

"I think Nathan will be fine, anyway," she said. "What are you two doing for the holidays?"

"Not sure yet," I said. "He's going to visit his family, but... things didn't go so well last time I saw them."

That was putting it mildly.

"If you don't have plans, you can always join my family for Christmas dinner," she said.

"Thanks." I smiled. "Nathan will be back before the new year, anyway."

Despite the reminders everywhere, I kept forgetting how soon the holidays were... mostly because another event stood in the way. The solstice. The chance to see my Dad—or not. Assuming he got in touch.

Silence didn't mean bad news... right?

————

I tossed and turned all night, and when I finally dozed off, I dreamt Nathan and I were hauled off to a prison under a giant mushroom by a group of hunters who turned out to be gargoyle shifters. Then Sky transformed into a massive pixie and flew us away.

Sometimes my subconscious worried me, to say the least.

I stopped by the local police office on the way to work that morning, only to find the place overflowing with werewolves demanding to speak to Steve. The place was staffed entirely by gargoyles, including the fancy new jail next door, but not enough to handle the whole leading werewolf pack. If I waited for them all to leave, I'd be late for work, so I reluctantly turned away and headed for Dritch & Co's office.

There, I found a morose-looking Callie sitting at the reception desk. Her blond hair hung lank on either side of her tired face, and huge bags lurked under her eyes. "Oh, hey, Blair."

"Hey." I halted beside the desk. "I saw a lot of the pack members at the police station. Did they find any more clues last night?"

"No," she said. "My dad's been trying to keep everyone in order, but Claude is refusing to listen to reason."

"Does he really think Nathan did it?" I kept my voice low, fervently hoping the others hadn't heard yet.

"I don't know," she said. "I think he's innocent, for the record."

"He is," I said firmly. "It's absurd that anyone would

suspect him at all. I take it the search for the weapon didn't work out?"

"No." She rested her head on her folded arms. "You'll have to ask Rob. My dad doesn't like me getting involved in family disputes, so I wasn't there when it all went down. Last I heard, he was heading to the police station to stop Claude from doing something reckless."

I remembered Claude implying that he thought his uncle wouldn't be the pack's leader for much longer. Maybe he'd been overexaggerating out of grief and anger, but it made me uneasy to think of Nathan turning into a pawn in a pack argument between family members.

Unfortunately, Claude was right on one count—the killer was likely a hunter, who'd come close enough to the border to attack an innocent person. I could only assume Nathan knew who to report them to, or we'd be looking at a worse problem than an argument between competing wolves. The chief had threatened to take his people and leave town once before when he'd believed the pack to be in danger. This time, though, certain members of the pack didn't seem to trust their own chief's judgement, let alone anyone else's.

"I hope they get to the bottom of it, soon." I headed into the office to join my fellow teammates.

Rob had left a mug of coffee on my desk, as usual, but lacked his warm smile. "Hey, Blair."

"Hey," I said. "Late night?"

"Pretty late," he said. "The chief had us combing the forest until it was too dark to see our own noses. And werewolves have bloody good night vision."

"The chief asked you to?" I frowned. "I wouldn't have

thought the killer would have hidden in the woods with the pack on full alert."

The murderer might be miles away by now, but it was beyond me to tell what the chief was thinking at the moment. He'd asked for *my* expertise, for a start.

Rob shrugged. "Maybe, but the chief's suspicious about how quickly the killer disappeared. Besides, it was the only way to shut my brother up. I figured if we found a weapon, it wouldn't be hard to sniff out whose finger-prints were on it."

Not Nathan's. I hadn't seen or heard from him since yesterday, but even if he hadn't been locked up as a suspect, I'd bet he'd been dealing with Steve all night. I hoped the grumpy gargoyle had sent out teams to search the fields beyond the town for any signs of our rogue hunter. After all, the quickest way to prove Nathan's inno-cence was to find the real culprit.

"What do you know about the victim?" I asked.

"Not much," said Rob. "Alec and I were never friends. I didn't really hang out with that crowd. But he was a decent guy. He used to be the pack band's drummer, but I guess he quit recently."

He was in the band?

Alissa and I had made the mistake of going to watch the werewolves' infamous band at the New Moon cafe during my first week in town, and the experience fell somewhere between an amateur talent show and a car crash. At the time, I'd sworn I'd rather listen to a chorus of sirens than go near them again.

Lizzie walked into the office, and the printer broke into a rendition of *God Rest Ye, Merry Gentlemen* in welcome. As normality descended, I moved the murder case to the back of my mind. Bethan entered the office and sat down, and Veronica walked in a moment later.

The boss clapped her hands loudly enough to make us jump in our seats. "Right, everyone. No slacking, no gossiping, no getting distracted. We need results."

"All right," said Bethan, looking slightly alarmed. "We're on it. Whatever 'it' is."

"Good." Veronica sauntered out, letting the door swing shut behind her. "Callie, stop sleeping on the desk. We've got work to do."

Callie's mumbled apology was cut off by the sound of the printer singing the chorus of *Silent Night.*

Lizzie looked up from her computer. "There's already been a cancellation. Turns out one of yesterday's candidates was three goblins in a trench coat pretending to be a wizard."

I blinked. "Who vetted that guy?"

"He sounded normal on the phone," Bethan said. "How'd they find out?"

"The extra arms gave it away."

"Well, of course they did." Between clients and the boss's inexplicable mood swings, it was a wonder we hadn't all gone as mad as the printer. "Does anyone know why the boss is so set on us making these imaginary targets?"

"No," said Bethan. "She won't tell me a thing."

It was hard to focus on clients with the werewolf murder and Nathan's predicament weighing on my mind, but the last thing I needed was to end up behind schedule on top of everything else. The morning dragged on endlessly despite my best efforts to distract myself.

"Interviewee here," came Callie's voice from the reception area. "For you, Blair."

I frowned. "I didn't invite anyone for an interview, did I?"

Oh, no. There was only one person it might be.

Sure enough, a moment later, Erin walked into the office. Like yesterday, she wore muddy boots, jeans and a ragged jacket. "Hey, Blair."

"Hi." Aware of the others watching me in confusion, I invited her into the same interview room as yesterday. "Sorry last night didn't go as planned. Um, I'm not sure Steve will give you an interview to work for the police. Since, you know, your brother is a possible murder suspect."

I'd been waiting for the chance to talk face to face about her fellow hunters, but I'd have preferred not to do it where the others could overhear. Particularly Rob, with his enhanced werewolf hearing.

"Nathan isn't in jail," said Erin. "He told me Steve has him under close watch for the duration of the investigation to stop the werewolves kicking up a fuss, but he isn't an official suspect."

It would have saved me a lot of worrying if he'd told *me* that. "They don't know you're in town?"

"It's not like I announced I was coming here," she said. "What was I supposed to do, run through the forest with a loudspeaker, saying, *Don't worry, I'm not a hunter anymore?*"

I grimaced. "You know there are two werewolves working in this office, right? Including the chief's daughter?"

Her face fell. "I had to speak to someone. It was driving me mad, and you're the only person in Fairy Falls

I know except my brother. I can't talk to *him* in person until the police let him go home."

Hmm. If I admitted it, the best thing she could do was leave town before she became a suspect herself, but she probably wouldn't appreciate the suggestion. Besides, most people in town wouldn't realise she and Nathan were related, though it would help if she dressed a bit less like a hunter.

"Please tell me you didn't know another hunter might be near town," I said to her.

"No. I swear I didn't."

True.

"All right. Just checking." I took in a breath. "Since it does look like the werewolf was shot by someone carrying a hunter's weapon, it seems unlikely that a non-hunter stumbled upon one of their guns by accident and happened to shoot a werewolf with it. Do you know anyone who might have reason to target the pack?"

"Not at all." She shook her head. "Hunters don't kill except as a last resort. The rules are clear."

"I've met hunters who don't follow the rules before."

Surprise flared in her expression. "Who?"

Hadn't her brother told her about Sleepy, Dopey and Grumpy? "A group of them worked with a local criminal who wanted to displace the town's witch council. I heard they were fired by the hunters, but they have a grudge against me, and they aren't very bright."

"I think Nathan may have mentioned the incident," she said. "But I don't know them personally."

True. "They already wandered onto werewolf territory at least once," I explained. "Like I said… not smart. I know it's a lot to ask, but would you be able to call the local hunters' branch and find out if the three of them have been seen in the area?"

"I bet my brother already has," she said. "Anyway, if they were fired, they'd have been forced to return their weapons. I didn't leave the hunters on good terms, so I don't think they'd appreciate me calling them."

"Might they have sent someone after you?" I asked.

A heartbeat passed. "No, and if they did, they wouldn't shoot someone in cold blood to make a point. They know I'd never come back to the fold if I found out."

True. "All right. But the odds of it *not* being one of them are pretty low, just going by the murder weapon."

"I know." Her hands clenched on either side of her seat. "I really don't know who did it, Blair, I promise." Her voice rang with sincerity.

"I believe you."

She lifted her chin. "Thanks, Blair. Guess I picked a bad time to go job hunting in the paranormal world, eh?"

Job hunting. Right. I was supposed to be interviewing her, and considering Veronica's bizarre new fixation on targets, the others wouldn't be thrilled that we'd spent the last ten minutes chatting instead.

"Uh, are there any other areas you'd like to work in?" I asked, in a clumsy attempt to steer the conversation back on track.

"I always wondered if I was cut out to go into tourism," she said in thoughtful tones. "This town doesn't have a tourism office, does it?"

I blinked. "Now that you mention it... no. I guess we don't get many people coming here from outside."

I was one of the few exceptions, and my arrival had caused a stir, to say the least.

"It's a nice location," said Erin. "I'm surprised."

"I guess there's a few people in town who don't get along with outsiders." Like most of the wolf pack, a lot of the elves, the vampires... okay, more than a few people. And then there was all the secrecy around Fairy Falls and the lake. "But mostly it's because we can't invite non-paranormals in, and I guess not enough paranormals travel to make it worth setting up a tourism office."

Erin pursed her lips. "Seems a shame."

"I can look for other nearby towns which have tourism offices," I added. "We don't just offer employment options inside Fairy Falls itself."

"Oh, I'm not sure I'm interested," she said. "I much prefer it here."

"Erin." I fidgeted in my seat. "You do know the hunters have this town marked on their list, right? You won't permanently escape them if you choose to stay here."

An emotion I couldn't read entered her eyes. "I know. I'd leave the area if I wanted to escape them altogether. I just want them to stop giving me orders, that's all."

True... and yet I was sure that wasn't all. Employment alone couldn't have driven her to pick Fairy Falls as her new home. She'd certainly seemed to enjoy the time she'd spent here, but I'd assumed she'd used it as an excuse to leave the hunters, not the main reason.

"I can find a list of people who are open to hiring someone without magic," I said. "That's all I can do for now."

Erin got to her feet. "I know you're worried about my brother. If I can, I'll tell him to get in touch with you."

He shouldn't need prompting. Most likely, Steve wouldn't give him a break. If Erin didn't know anything about the hunters' involvement, then I shouldn't feel guilty for keeping her presence in town from the law enforcement. After all, she hadn't lied, nor was she an active hunter.

"Thanks," I said. "It's appreciated."

I waved Erin off and steeled myself to spend the day working at twice the speed as usual to make up for the time I'd lost. When I re-entered the office, it was to find Rob was nowhere in sight.

"He went home," said Bethan in explanation. "Had to deal with some family emergency. What is going on?"

I waited until I saw Erin pass by the office window before saying, "Someone was murdered last night. A werewolf."

"Oh." Bethan's gaze went to the window. "I thought something was wrong. Callie's gone home, too, so one of us might be called to work on the front desk. Was the victim someone in their family?"

"Not a relation of theirs, but you know, the pack is like a big family."

Or it had been, anyway, before this odd new rift between the chief and his nephew.

I didn't want to bring up Nathan in front of my colleagues. If he hadn't actually been arrested, then he'd help the police get to the bottom of the case and call the hunters to find out if any of their people had wandered out of bounds lately. It wasn't fair to Veronica or the others to spend the day with my head in the clouds when they needed me to help handle clients.

And yet it was hard not to wonder if the hunters had been looking for Erin. Surely, they hadn't come to town with the intention of shooting a werewolf—but what had their real goal been?

———

After work, I headed to the police station, finding it werewolf-free. Inside, Steve stood talking to Clare, the receptionist, while there were no signs of Nathan anywhere.

"Where is Nathan?" I asked Steve.

"Busy," he replied tersely. "If you want to speak to him, call him outside of work hours."

"He's been there since late yesterday evening," I pointed out. "I just wanted to make sure you hadn't locked him up."

"We haven't," said Clare. "He isn't listed as a suspect."

"Then why has he been here for the last day?" I asked.

"Not that it's any of your business, but Nathan has the expertise on the hunters," growled Steve. "He is now head of the case. If you want to know more, I'd suggest you ask him yourself, but not while he's at my office. That clear?"

Then why hadn't he responded to my messages yet? He'd texted Erin, and it wasn't typical of him to refrain from getting in touch with me, especially when he must know I was worried about him.

From the expression on the police chief's face, he didn't want me shoving my way into the investigation. If I mentioned Erin, he might lock *her* up with no trial—unlike Nathan, she wasn't useful to him. I was better off going it alone.

After all, I did know one place the werewolves would be hanging out tonight.

———

"No luck?" said Alissa as I let myself into the flat.

"Steve wouldn't let me in. Said Nathan was 'busy'." I rolled my eyes. "I bet he doesn't tell Nathan I came by, so I can't blame him for not texting me. I just wish I could do something."

The werewolves needed an objective outsider's perspective. That, or a dose of the potion they gave their young werewolves at the full moon, which had even successfully turned the grumpy former Head Witch into a positively mellow person. For a short time, at least.

"Blair, I doubt taking over Steve's investigation will do anything but make him mad at you," she said.

"That's not what I was thinking," I said. "Erin's in town and I don't think she's involved, but I do think the police are missing a few clues. Either I fly over the forest to the border and look around…"

"With angry werewolves sniffing for trouble."

"…or I go and question them upfront again."

"And those same werewolves will kick you off their territory."

"Not if I don't go to their territory," I said. "We all know where the werewolves spend their evenings."

Alissa frowned. "You have got to be kidding me."

"I'll owe you," I said. "I'll pay for all your groceries for the rest of the month."

Alissa's expression didn't waver.

"And clean up after both the cats."

No change.

"And I'll bring snacks to your shifts at the hospital. Even the night-time ones."

She sighed. "All right. But you owe me, big time."

5

Alissa and I made our way to the New Moon pub later that evening. While part of me hoped that the werewolves had found an alternative form of entertainment for the sake of everyone who had to listen, the band members seemed permanently attached to their instruments when they weren't running around the forest. Rob had mentioned Alec had once been the band's drummer, so I had a decent chance of finding someone to speak to who might know what he'd been doing the night he'd died.

The werewolves' infamous hangout was almost exclusively attended by shifters. Or shifters who were particularly tolerant of obnoxiously loud noise, anyway. The sound of the bass made the entire street vibrate, while the vocalist sounded like he was howling in pain. Or possibly screaming at someone to get out of the pub. With the werewolves, it was anyone's guess.

The New Moon itself was pleasant enough, with

comfy chairs grouped around wooden tables, but the musical equivalent of a car being crushed into scrap metal somewhat marred the atmosphere. Even with one of their members recently murdered, the band played their hearts out on the wooden stage at the back of the pub.

Alissa's ex, Bryan, was the first to notice us. He stopped in the middle of a song, his guitar twanging to a halt, and the vocalist turned around to yell at the drummer when he fell off his stool. They must have found a replacement for Alec, then.

I rose to my feet as Bryan jumped off the stage, ready to step in if he started hassling Alissa again. Alissa might be dating someone else, but her ex was notoriously persistent and had only backed off after Alissa had threatened to have him arrested for intentionally trying to cause her a mild injury in order to stop her from being targeted by a killer.

"What are you doing in here?" he asked.

"Just soaking in the ambience," said Alissa.

Or drowning in it.

"I hoped to speak with the band members," I explained. "The pack chief wanted me to look into Alec's death, but Steve and the police ordered me to leave your territory before I could finish asking questions, and I didn't want to come back into the forest without an explanation. I was told Alec played in the band?"

"Yeah, he was our drummer." He shot a disgruntled look at the shaggy-haired man who'd toppled off the stool and dropped both drumsticks in the process.

"Who are you?" The lead singer marched across the stage and returned his microphone to the stand, setting off a wave of static that must have been audible to every animal in town.

"I'm Blair," I said. "I was told Alec used to play the drums in your band, and given his recent death, the pack chief asked me to find out more."

The lead singer—whose blond hair suggested he was some relation of the chief's—scowled. "The chief didn't tell *me* about getting anyone from outside the pack involved."

"He asked me to question the whole pack." It wasn't exactly a lie, even though the chief hadn't specifically told me to come here. "Since I can tell when anyone isn't being truthful, he thought I might be able to help."

"Blair can do a better job than Steve," added Alissa, who kept both eyes on Bryan as though daring him to come closer. He suddenly became very interested in cleaning his guitar.

"I doubt it," the lead singer said. "Besides, it's obvious what happened. One of those hunters decided to come to town and start a fight with the pack."

"I don't know who did it," I said. "But I'm here to help. Alec used to be your drummer, didn't he?"

"He did, but if you're looking for gossip, we aren't like you witches. We don't betray our own."

"I'm not here for gossip," I said. "The chief wants to know how he ended up alone in the woods when he was shot."

"Beats me," grunted the werewolf. "The night he died, I was here with the rest of the band, rehearsing with the new drummer. By the time we got back to the forest, there were gargoyles everywhere."

True. If he and the rest of the band had all been here,

then they all had alibis. They also wouldn't have seen the killer.

"Did Alec often go wandering alone in the forest?" I asked.

"I have no idea," he said. "I don't care about what the band members do in their spare time. He didn't do anything to warrant being slaughtered by those hunters, that's for sure."

"I'm sure he didn't." The band members wouldn't know who the killer was, but perhaps they might be able to shed some light on Alec's actions before he died. "When did he leave the band?"

"We fired him last week," he said. "He was late to every other rehearsal and didn't turn up to the rest, and we only kept him because we couldn't find a good replacement."

It sounded like they were still having that issue, judging by drummer's inability to keep hold of his drumsticks. It couldn't be easy to find someone willing to commit to hours of rehearsals and playing every night of the week to an indifferent audience.

The sound of static wailed from Bryan's guitar. "C'mon, Joe," he said to the lead singer. "If we don't get on with it, we'll be here all night. Let the newbie try again."

"Right, right," said Joe. "Waste of bloody time… he was the best we could get on short notice."

Jumping back onto the stage, he picked up the microphone again. He hadn't told me to leave, so I re-joined Alissa, who'd bought cocktails for both of us and placed them on a table near the stage.

"They contain mood-boosters," she whispered in my ear. "They'll make the noise bearable, if not drown it out."

I could have used an earplug charm instead, but that

wouldn't help with my questioning. I took a long sip of the cocktail, which sent a heady buzz through my veins that banished my headache and replaced it with a pleasant humming sensation.

After a long stretch of crashing noises that may or may not have been music, the band stopped playing when the drummer hit the cymbal with such force that his drumstick flew across the room and landed in someone's drink.

"Go and get that, you moron." The lead singer replaced the microphone on the stand and glared at the drummer. Then he spotted Alissa and me. "You're still here?"

Considering my boyfriend's freedom might depend on my solving this murder—yes, I am. "Do you know if the gargoyles managed to find any traces of the killer around the border? If they tracked them by air, the hunters couldn't have gone far."

"No," he said. "Those gargoyles are short-sighted, and hunters are experts at hiding. They found no weapon either, or so I'm told. If I were you, I'd look to your own first. I heard there's a new hunter sniffing around town. What's her name, Erin?"

He knows? I supposed it shouldn't be a surprise. Erin was not the subtle type, and as I'd noted before, Fairy Falls didn't get a large number of visitors from outside town. The werewolves made a habit of keeping an eye on the hunters, too, which made the recent events all the stranger.

"She's an ex-hunter, and she's not a suspect," I said. "She's here looking for work, and she doesn't even know where the pack lives in the forest, as far as I know."

"I don't trust a single person who worked for them," he growled. "They shot Alec from behind when he was in human form. They didn't even give him the chance to fight back."

"From behind?" I echoed. "How'd you know he was in human form when he was shot, if there were no witnesses?"

"Because nobody would dare to shoot one of us in shifted form," he said. "They'd be dead before they raised the gun. As for why they shot him from behind, if they hadn't, he'd have seen the scumbag coming."

The drummer climbed back onto the stage and accidentally kicked the microphone stand over.

With an exasperated sigh, Joe put it the right way up. "Right. Let's start again from the beginning."

The drummer groaned. "It's the fifteenth time today."

"Maybe if you put your back into it, then I wouldn't need to ask you to keep starting over, would I?"

I had the distinct impression they were going to be one drummer short again before long. With a crash of cymbals, the band launched into an energetic sequence, while I did my best not to look like I was being repeatedly hit over the head with a broomstick. Alissa, meanwhile, wore the expression she usually reserved for dealing with difficult patients. We ordered a second round of cocktails, and it wasn't until the band stopped playing in the middle of the song that I noticed the shadowy figure standing behind our table.

The lead singer continued growling into the microphone, but his fellow band members had put their instruments down, their attention on the new arrival.

A tall man stood silently in the dim light in front of the stage, looking markedly out of place in his smart suit. He had dark skin and hair and moved with the silent swiftness of a vampire. A vampire *librarian,* that is. A vampire librarian in a werewolf pub.

Alissa looked down and mouthed, "Oh, no."

What in the world was Samuel doing here? I'd never heard of a vampire setting foot in a pub for werewolves, given their long-standing feud. Despite being outnumbered, he didn't look frightened as he approached the bar and spoke to a bemused-looking bartender. *He's seriously ordering a drink? At a werewolf pub? They serve steaks, not blood cocktails.*

"Did you by any chance tell him you'd be here tonight?" I whispered to Alissa.

"No." She stared at the back of his head, her expression as dazed as the bartender's. "I think he must have seen us come in and decided to make sure the werewolves didn't pick a fight."

"If anything, they're more likely to tear *him* to pieces."

The werewolves onstage conversed in low voices as the vampire walked over to our table and set down his drink. Then he pulled a small bottle of red liquid from his pocket and tipped it into the glass. It was not tomato juice.

Alissa and I stared open-mouthed as Samuel sat down and smiled. His teeth didn't appear pointed, but everyone knew he wore an illusion charm so as not to scare the students who visited the university library where he worked. He sat there, sipping his cocktail, as though he wasn't in mortal danger. Or immortal danger, depending on how you looked at it.

"I have to admit, Alissa, I didn't take you to be a fan of this... music," he said.

Alissa closed her eyes and then opened them again.

"I'm just here to help Blair with something. We were going to leave in a minute."

"Oh, don't leave on my account." The vampire eyed Bryan with dislike and took a long drink of his blood-red cocktail. "I'll wait for you to finish your questioning."

"Please don't read my thoughts." I glanced at the stage, where the band continued to watch the vampire instead of resuming their act. "Alissa's only here to help me. As moral support. But I think we're done with the questioning anyway."

Before any of us could move, the door slid open and another tall man dressed in black walked in. His chalk-white face resembled a waxwork model, his black hair was slicked back, and his suit was impeccably tailored to fit his tall form. He moved like smoke shaped like a human, so swift and silent that he reached our table before any of the band members noticed his presence. Judging by the expressions on the werewolves' faces, no vampire had ever been near their pub as long as it existed, let alone their leader.

"Samuel." Vincent beckoned to the younger vampire.

Samuel rose to his feet without a word, leaving his cocktail on the table. Alissa jumped up, her body tensing as though ready to run.

"We don't allow vampires in our establishment," said the lead singer into the microphone, his words echoing off the walls of the pub.

"That's news to me," said Vincent. "Perhaps you should put up a sign on your door to prevent any confusion?"

Vincent might be outnumbered by people who could turn into wolves in the blink of an eye, but the elder vampire still acted as though he had the upper hand.

I grabbed Alissa's arm. "Let's leave them to it."

Alissa, thankfully, agreed, and we backed toward the door as the werewolves closed in on the new arrivals. When the howling started, the two of us escaped into the night.

"What in the world was that about?" I asked Alissa. "Did you know he was going to follow you?"

"Of course not." She shook her head. "I don't know how he even knew I was there."

"He's a vampire," I said, which was explanation enough in itself. "As for Vincent, I didn't know he frequented the local pubs."

"Nor me." Alissa slipped on the cobblestones, catching her balance on a lamp post. "Whoa, those cocktails are strong. I forgot they're made for werewolves' higher metabolisms."

I took an unsteady step forward, and the world dipped like a seesaw. "So did I, but I somehow doubt Vincent went in there for a drink."

"I guess he must keep tabs on the other vampires," Alissa said.

"And he comes to collect them if they do something stupid like starting a fight with a pack of wolves," I added.

"Can you blame him?" Alissa tottered down the street. "I imagine seeing the two of us go alone into a werewolves' pub right after one of them died worried him."

"He didn't have to make things worse by sitting in front of the stage and adding his own supply of blood to his drink," I pointed out.

She grimaced. "I'll have a word with him. Did you get anything useful from talking to the band members?"

"The lead singer said Alec often skipped rehearsals or showed up late, so they fired him."

"Ah." Her brow pinched. "Guess he wasn't committed to his role in the band, but that doesn't mean there's any link between that and his death. Sounds like he was just unlucky."

"So are they." I winced at the sound of crashing and howling from inside the pub, which suggested Vincent was having an interesting night. "The lead singer also said Alec was shot in the back while in human form. So it sounds like the killer didn't feel threatened."

Which meant the killer hadn't cared if his death looked like self-defence or not. But was that simple hunter arrogance, or something else?

"Shot in the back?" said Alissa. "While fleeing?"

"I don't know, but I always thought werewolves didn't run from a fight," I said. "I know a silver bullet would have killed him either way, but if he'd felt threatened, he would have shifted, right?"

Alissa nodded. "You're right. He can't have seen the attacker coming."

"Also, they knew he was a werewolf even though he hadn't shifted," I added. "So either the killer was familiar with the pack's territory or came here expecting to be attacked. A hunter wouldn't shoot a human."

Her expression turned serious. "Then it was premeditated. Do the police know that?"

"They should, considering they talked to half the pack today," I said. "I assume Nathan does, too."

I still hadn't heard from him. Worry began to seep through the buzzing effects of the alcohol. Either Steve had lied, and he really was holding Nathan hostage until he solved the crime—or, for whatever reason, Nathan didn't *want* to get in touch with me. He didn't want me to be involved in the investigation.

We turned to head home, and the howls of angry werewolves pursued us through the night. It did not seem like a good omen.

6

The one upside to the magical cocktail was that I slept like the dead. The major downside became obvious when I woke up to the sound of my alarm pounding into my skull like a drill. I groaned and pulled the covers over my head, but Sky prodded me in the side of the face as though to say, *Tough. You have to get up for work.*

I didn't typically drink on weeknights, but the werewolves' awful music had led me to forget to bother with a hangover-repelling cocktail and had instead fallen straight into bed when I'd got home.

I took some painkillers and walked to work with my head swimming as though I was underwater. Callie raised an eyebrow at me as I walked into the wall instead of the door on the way into the office.

"Goodness, Blair," she said. "If I didn't know where you were last night, then I'd say you should probably go home. I don't think the boss will accept werewolf cocktails as an excuse, though."

I groaned. "I guess the whole pack knows what went down at the New Moon last night. Believe it or not, Alissa and I had no idea the vampires would show up."

"Luckily for both of you, whoever told my dad the story left your names out of it," said Callie. "What were you thinking?"

"I was told Alec used to play in the werewolves' band." I rubbed my forehead. "Guess I overcompensated with the cocktails I used to shut out the noise while I questioned the lead singer."

The door to our office opened, and Rob leaned out into the reception area. "Thought I heard your voice, Blair. Come in and tell me all about how you brought a group of vampires to start a brawl in the New Moon. I'm disappointed I missed it."

I stifled another groan. "I didn't bring the vampires with me. They came by themselves."

"Joking, joking," said Rob, his easy manner back as though nothing had happened. "I added a hangover cure to your coffee, by the way. It should be good for at least eight hours."

"If I'm to get through work today, I'll need it." I entered the office and more or less fell into my seat. "Thanks."

Rob handed me a steaming mug. "I'd happily make you coffee every day if you can repeat the New Moon incident again when I'm actually there."

I took a long sip of coffee, not caring when it burned my tongue. "I didn't see most of it. Alissa and I got out of there as soon as things turned violent, so we didn't see how it ended."

"The werewolves trashed the place," said Rob.

"You mean the vampires?" I put my mug down between two stacks of papers.

"Nope, the werewolves," he said. "The vamps moved too fast for the pack to catch them, so the whole bar got wrecked in the process."

"It's probably for the best you weren't there," I said. "Vincent seemed to be looking for a fight. Alissa and I were just unlucky bystanders."

"Who shouldn't have been in there," he added. "Not that I'm complaining. They'll be telling that story at parties for months. What did Joe have to say, then?"

"He said Alec skipped band skipped rehearsals so much that they fired him," I said. "Does that sound right?"

"Wouldn't surprise me," he said. "Like I said, I didn't really know the guy. We haven't spoken since we were at university."

I'd forgotten he'd studied at the town's only university —which was one of the reasons I'd hired him as our fourth team member to begin with. Then again, my brain wasn't exactly operating at full capacity today. Alec might have been at the border for any reason, but considering he'd been shot in the back while in human form, the odds of a hunter *not* being responsible were pretty low.

I checked my phone. Not a single word from Nathan. No messages, no missed calls, though I could have slept through an earthquake last night. I could only assume he hadn't heard about my involvement in the incident at the New Moon or was too busy to contact me.

The thought made my headache come screaming back, so I drank the rest of my coffee and tried to turn my attention to the tasks of the day.

Rob's hangover cure lasted through work, but by evening, my headache returned with a vengeance, stabbing me between the eyes all the way to the witches' headquarters. I walked inside, squinting against the ceiling lights and wishing I could dim them without Rita noticing. I doubted she'd be pleased to know what I'd been up to yesterday evening, so I'd just have to stick it out. *Please let it be a simple theory lesson.*

"Today, we'll be trying your first lesson in syncing spells," Rita said to Rebecca and me. "It ought to help you use the sceptre, Rebecca, and as an added bonus, you'll get in some preparation for your next exam. No need to look so alarmed, Blair, it's easy enough. Both of you, copy me. If you do the movements correctly, nothing should go amiss as long as your wand-work is correct."

It might have been easy if my head didn't feel like a watermelon that had been dropped off a roof, but on the first attempt, I dyed the walls blue. Then a glitter shower drenched all three of us. When Rita switched to levitation charms in despair, I accidentally turned off the lights, resulting in Rebecca panicking and dropping the sceptre. A flood of purple light filled the room and my feet left the ground, my body flipping over in mid-air. My head spun with nausea and it was all I could do not to throw up on the floor. Using my wings to steady myself, I landed back on my feet and clumsily restored the lights to their former state.

"Really, Blair," said Rita, handing Rebecca her sceptre back. "What's the matter with you today?"

"It's been a long day at work," I mumbled. "I've just been distracted lately. Sorry."

Rebecca frowned sideways at me but didn't comment.

Rita sighed. "Well, try it once more. And Rebecca, don't let Blair distract you."

Thoroughly chagrined, I waved my wand more carefully this time. My spell hit the book I'd been aiming for, but instead of flying into the air, it flew sideways into the book Rebecca was supposed to be levitating. Rebecca's spell missed the book and hit the desk instead, which flew into the neighbouring wall with such force that the teacher in the room next door yelled something unintelligible.

"Sorry!" Rebecca waved the sceptre, flustered. A jet of light shot from the end, striking the wall with an audible cracking sound.

When the light cleared, we looked in horror through the newly created hole in the wall to the students in the classroom next door.

"Hey, isn't that the fairy witch?" one of them said.

Rita sighed. "I'll fix the wall. You two, leave. You can tell Madame Grey exactly how that happened."

I followed Rebecca out of the classroom, my head drooping as much as Rebecca's. Worse, Madame Grey didn't answer when we knocked on the door to her office, leaving us standing awkwardly in the lobby while the sound of students giggling issued from the classroom with the hole in the wall.

"Sorry," I said. "That was my fault."

"No, it was mine," Rebecca said. "I didn't have a strong enough grip on the sceptre. I'm not good enough to use its magic."

"Of course you are," I said. "I have no excuses. I was just tired and not paying attention."

"Neither do I," she said quietly. "I'm a failure. The sceptre made a mistake when it picked me."

"Of course you aren't a failure," I said. "The bullies aren't saying things to you again, are they?"

"No, they haven't for a while." She stared at the carpeted floor. "Everyone keeps asking me to perform magic for them and they don't understand why I still use my wand to cast spells at school. It's only a matter of time before they find out I can't use the sceptre at all."

"You can," I insisted. "You might not have full control over it yet, but when you do, you'll impress them. Wait and see."

"It's been months." Tears trembled on the ends of her eyelashes. "Maybe in a year I'll be good enough, but I don't have a year. I know Rita and Madame Grey keep having to make excuses for me to the other covens. I heard her and Rita talking… they said I'm going to be *tested* by the region's inspectors, to make sure I'm worthy of being Head Witch. They're coming here before the end of term."

"Tested?" I echoed. "In what way?"

"Like an exam." She looked away.

Before I could say a word, the front doors opened and Nathan walked into the entrance hall. His eyes widened at the sight of me. "Blair?"

"Fancy meeting you here." The words came out more caustically than I'd intended, thanks to a combination of my hangover and the far more potent cocktail of emotions churning inside me. Shame, anger, relief, sadness, worry… and despite it all, the usual jolt of happiness I felt whenever I saw his face.

"Is Madame Grey in?" said Nathan.

He didn't even come here to see me? "Not at the moment. Steve let you go, then? I thought he had you on a tight leash?"

He frowned. "Blair—the pack sighted a hunter outside the forest. I'd prefer to have backup with me when I go after them."

My heart plunged into my shoes. "They found the killer?"

"I don't know." He pushed the front door open again. "Blair—I promise I'll explain everything later."

"Like hell." I turned to Rebecca. "I'm sorry, but I have to see what's going on out there. I'll come and talk to Madame Grey when she's back."

"Of course you have to go," she said. "I'll see you later."

"Sorry—thanks." I hurried after Nathan, who was already walking away. "Hey! What in the world is wrong with you? Don't I at least get a hello?"

"I'm sorry, Blair." He slowed his pace—marginally. "I never wanted you involved in this."

"In what, exactly?" I said. "The murder investigation, or with the hunters? Or your life?"

That brought him to a halt. "What? Why would you think that?"

"Are you kidding me?" I said. "You've been ignoring my messages ever since you nearly got arrested. I know you're busy with the investigation, but you clearly have time to tell Erin what you're up to while she tries to hire my company to get a job, knowing full well that I could get fired or arrested if the pack *or* the hunters find out." I sucked in a deep breath. "And I went to that bloody were-wolf pub last night and got drunk on their stupid cock-tails to help with this case—nearly getting caught in a vampire-werewolf brawl in the process, I might add—and you won't even stop to say hi."

Nathan, whose brows had crept higher with every word, opened his mouth. "Blair... wow."

"Wow," I said weakly. "Also, I think I might throw up. Fair warning."

"Don't you have a hangover cure?"

"It wore off." I rubbed my forehead. "I know, I shouldn't have gone out on a weeknight, but is it any more irresponsible than ditching your girlfriend when she was worried about your well-being?"

"I didn't know you were worried," he said. "I told Erin I was fine in the hopes that she'd pass on the message to you, and then I'd be able to explain everything when I had a free moment. And when I'm not being watched."

"Can't you ditch Steve?" I rubbed my temples, my headache easing a little as some of the weight disappeared from my shoulders.

He shook his head. "It's complicated. And I really do have to run. A hunter was sighted just north of the border, and if the werewolves get there first..."

"You expected to outrun the werewolves from the other side of town?" I shook my head at him. "Look, I can fly there and check. If there *is* a hunter, I'll use my glamour to sneak up on them before the werewolves get near."

Maybe then he'd let me stay involved in this case. Besides, it had been too long since I'd had the chance to exercise my fairy powers.

His mouth pressed into a line. "Blair, I won't let you put yourself in danger."

"Werewolves can't see through glamour. And I move fast."

I couldn't promise I wouldn't throw up on someone, but if the hunter was responsible for the murder, it was the least of what he deserved. If not, it was better than being torn apart by angry werewolves.

Nathan started to protest, but something in my expression must have convinced him. "Okay. I'll be waiting for you."

"I'll hold you to that."

I snapped my fingers and transformed into my fairy form. I looked more or less the same as I did as a human, except my ears were more pointed and a pair of wings sprouted from my shoulders. I shed a cloud of glitter as I flew into the sky, snapping my fingers again as I did so. At once, the glamour rendered me invisible, glitter and all.

If the werewolves were already chasing down the hunter, I'd need to be at my highest speed. I forgot all about my nauseated state as I flew uphill, through the town and over the forest towards the border. The setting sun painted the horizon in red streaks that highlighted the glimmering lake and the dark forest surrounding one side of it. I didn't see any fleeing figures in the fields beyond, but I spotted movement in the trees close to the west side of the forest and the university campus. Dipping lower, I aimed for a patch of trees on the edge of the border.

Then I came to a halt as I crashed headfirst into something sticky and net-like. Gasping for breath, I kicked out, finding my feet tangled in some kind of webbing. A giant spider's web? The forest contained elves, werewolves, and a wide range of other shifters, but no giant spiders, as far as I was aware.

I hung there breathlessly, my body suspended in the air, my limbs splayed in a frog-like manner. Grimacing, I tried to peel myself off the web, but it stuck fast to my skin and clothes, even my wings. All I managed to do was awkwardly bounce around like I was stuck on a trampoline made of superglue-coated string.

Now what? I couldn't reach my wand with my hands splayed out, or even snap my fingers to use glamour. I'd occasionally cast witch spells without a wand, but when I tried to wave my left hand, I succeeded only in tangling myself deeper in the sticky webbing. Squirming and kicking, I cursed my idiocy for volunteering to fly after the intruder. They were probably long gone, and now I'd fallen for someone's practical joke. Or I was about to become something's dinner.

Come on, Blair. Madame Grey would never let anything that eats humans live near town.

But had the hunters set up the trap? Or the werewolves? Surely not the latter, given the net's location. The quietness of the forest unnerved me, and so did the thought of being trapped here all night. If I yelled loudly enough, someone might come to rescue me... depending on whether they were friend or foe.

As images of giant spiders paraded across my mind, a small head popped up out of the bushes. It was the rat shifter I'd seen on my way to see the werewolves the other day, which came as a surprising relief. After all, there were worse people who might have caught me hanging around in a net.

"Hey," I said. "Can you give me a hand here?"

The rat shifter, Anton, started in surprise, peering up at me. "What are you doing in that tree?"

"I'm stuck in a net. Or a spiderweb. Not sure which." I tried to wave, but I couldn't even manage that. Up close, the net shone silvery like a massive spiderweb. How had I not seen it when I'd been in the air?

He shuffled closer and tugged on the edge of the web-like substance. "It's sticky."

"I know. Can you pull at that bit there?" I indicated with my chin, since my hands were tied together. "I might be able to reach my wand if you move my left hand. There... there."

I gave directions to the rat shifter, who tugged at the rope-like parts of the web attaching it to the trees.

"Make sure you don't get stuck, too," I said. "If you can't do it, can you fetch help? I'd prefer not to get stuck in here all night."

"My teeth are strong enough to bite through bark," he said, his voice muffled. "I'd rather avoid seeing the were-wolves again."

"I don't blame you." The web jostled me, coming looser around my left arm. I dragged my hand towards my pocket, inch by inch. "Were they chasing someone near the border?"

"Chasing?" Anton said. "I didn't see. If the werewolves are on a hunt, you want to be as far away as possible. They're not very kind to us small folk."

"I guess not." I wouldn't like to think what they might have done if they'd found me hanging around in the forest without a good reason for being there.

The rat shifter tugged on another of the rope-like

swathes of the web, loosening it from the tree. My left arm came free and I reached into my pocket to grab my wand.

With a wave, I cast a breaking spell. The net snapped and I dropped to the forest floor. I landed on my feet, my legs still tangled in sticky webs.

"Thanks," I said to the rat shifter, glad at least one person in the forest wasn't out to get me.

"Any time," he said. "I'd advise you not to linger too long in the forest. It's not safe."

"I know." I took a step forward. My foot stuck to the ground. Uh-oh.

Here we go again.

In the end, I had to pull off my shoes and use a cleaning spell on each of them to make the sticky webs vanished. Resigning myself to flying home covered in bits of web, I cleaned the stickiness from my wings and took flight above the trees.

Note to self: look before you land in future.

By the time I got back to the main part of town, it was dark. Worse, Nathan wasn't outside the witches' place any longer. Shedding bits of web, I walked into the lobby. If I couldn't find Nathan, I could at least find Madame Grey and explain that it was my fault Rebecca had accidentally blasted a hole in the wall during our lesson.

I knocked on her office door, but nobody responded. The sound of a classroom door opening came from behind me. I turned around and found myself faced with Rita.

"Hi," I said. "Did you manage to fix the hole in the wall?"

"Of course I did," she answered. "What is that stuck in

your hair?"

"Um… part of a net," I said. "Rebecca didn't get into trouble on my behalf, did she? We waited for Madame Grey, but she wasn't there. Then something urgent came up, and I had to leave. I got… tied up." *Literally.*

Rita gave me a long look. "No, she didn't get into trouble. Madame Grey is meeting with some of the other coven leaders at the moment, I believe. I expect you and Rebecca to both be on better form during your next lesson."

Rebecca's words from earlier came to mind. "Is she going to be… tested? On the sceptre, I mean?"

"Don't tell her, Blair," she said. "She's worried enough already."

Too late. "I think she's guessed. What does the test involve?"

She drew in a breath. "The representatives of the region's council are coming to assess the town. They usually meet the new Head Witch immediately after the ceremony, but since we haven't had a new sceptre wielder in decades and she's a child, there's been a lot of debates over how to handle her case. Since she's only Grade Three in witchcraft and it's unlikely that she'll reach a higher grade in time for their visit, they're adapting the assessment specifically for her. It's not going to be anything she doesn't already know."

"That's why you keep going over the same spells?" I asked.

"Yes, Blair, it is," she said. "I apologise for neglecting your own studies, but since the academy can't cover the extra lessons during school hours, I had no choice but to work them into our night classes."

"Don't worry about it," I said. "I'm fine. It's Rebecca I'm worried about. I think she's putting herself under a lot of pressure and it's making her confidence worse. When is this test?"

"On the winter solstice, I believe," she said.

"But... that's next week." The solstice also happened to be the one day the fairy prisoners from the hunters' jail were permitted supervised visits, yet I still hadn't heard from my dad about whether he'd be allowed to meet with me.

"I'm aware of that, Blair," she said. "The council will arrive in the morning and assess the town itself, and then Rebecca's test will take place in the afternoon."

"I thought the hunters already did an assessment," I said. "Why do the witch covens have to do the same?"

"This is different," she said. "The inspection is specifically focusing on the covens, the academy, and how our town as a whole is integrated. The hunters were only concerned with security and leadership, for the most part."

"You have to tell her. If it's in less than a week—"

"I planned to tell her after your lesson today, but given your poor performance, I decided it would be best to wait until later."

Guilt swamped me. I'd really screwed up. As for Rebecca? She had good reason to be intimidated for other reasons than feeling that she wasn't worthy of the sceptre. Maybe I should offer to give her a private tutoring session or three, to make it up to her.

My phone buzzed. I checked my messages, my heart swooping at the sight of Nathan's name. *Sorry I had to run off. Will talk later. Love, Nathan.*

7

Not a word came from Nathan that night, nor the following day at work. Once again, we were run off our feet all day, giving me little time to dwell on recent events.

When I left work, however, it was to find the wrong Harker sibling waiting outside. Erin smiled and waved at me.

"What in the world are you doing here?" I asked her. "If you wanted another interview, you're a bit late."

"Ah, no, I don't," she said. "I had an interview at a local bar today, and I'm waiting to hear back. I thought you'd want to know that my boyfriend is moving to town soon."

I frowned. "And he's an ex-hunter?"

"Uh. Still a hunter."

"Still a…" I stared at her in disbelief. "You mean *he's* the guy who was seen at the border yesterday?"

I walked down the road away from the office. This was not a conversation I wanted either of the werewolves working at Dritch & Co to overhear.

"I don't know," she said. "But he was supposed to meet me in town yesterday. I guess he was spotted and ran off. But he'd never use his weapon without good reason, and he wouldn't kill someone in cold blood."

True. "If you're wrong, you'll get into as much trouble as him," I warned. "He's lucky the werewolves didn't catch him. Or the gargoyles. What were both of you thinking?"

She looked down. "I didn't mean to get anyone into trouble, Blair."

"Does Nathan know?"

She bit her lip. "He knows we're together and that Buck is still a hunter. And he knows neither of us would ever hurt someone."

"The police don't," I said. "Erin, seriously, if there's something you know that the police don't—"

"I don't," she said vehemently. "Not about the murder, anyway. Or the hunters. I left months ago, Blair."

Her words rang with truth. But despite that, her boyfriend was *still* a hunter. Her assertions of his innocence didn't necessarily mean he *was,* only that she believed what he told her. My lie-sensing power did have its limitations.

To find out the truth, I'd need to speak to the man himself, but he was probably miles away by now. Thanks to my getting caught in that net, I'd missed my shot at catching up to yesterday's trespasser, if I'd ever been in with a chance to begin with.

Speaking of which. "Do the hunters ever use nets?"

"Nets?" she echoed. "What kind of nets?"

"I flew into one in the forest," I explained. "It was like a giant spiderweb. I got totally stuck and had to ask a rat shifter to help me get out."

Erin frowned. "The hunters did use nets like those, but I thought they went out of fashion years ago. I only know about them because my older brothers accidentally left one lying around the house when I was ten and I ended up getting stuck in it. I can't say I know how one would have ended up in the forest."

"It looked like someone put it there on purpose." Whoever had put the net there couldn't possibly have known I'd fly into it, but maybe Claude's claims that a hunter was intentionally picking off the pack members might have some merit after all.

"I assume there aren't," Erin continued. "For all you know, you might have an old retired hunter living in the forest. It happens sometimes. Can't settle into normal society, so they go and live with the wolves. Or the rats. I knew a guy who decided to join a local pack of wererabbits after retirement."

I rolled my eyes. "If someone's going around hanging nets up in the forest, that's a great way to get a different kind of early retirement."

"Hey, don't look at me," she said. "I hated those nets. You'll have to speak to my brother. He might be able to figure out who put it there."

"Can you at least message your boyfriend and tell him to stay away from the border until this mess is dealt with?" I said. "If he gets caught, both you *and* Nathan might wind up in custody. Not to mention me, my boss and colleagues might get into trouble for working with you, too."

"I messaged him," she said. "I'm sure they didn't catch him. It's not the first time he's had to outrun a wolf pack."

"Erin, that really isn't reassuring," I said. "Have you seen Nathan today?"

"No," she said. "Haven't heard from him. I guess the police still have him patrolling the border."

"Right. I'm going to fly into the forest and grab that net."

Even if Steve had locked Nathan in his office, he wouldn't be able to refuse to let me in if I had genuine evidence in my hands.

"By fly, you mean… fly?" Her eyes rounded with excitement. "Can you show me your wings? Just once, Blair. I won't ask again."

"Oh, all right." I snapped my fingers and turned into my fairy self, my wings beating behind my shoulders.

"Nice." She gave the wings an appreciative glance. "Bet that's a fun trick to use at parties."

I beat my wings, hovering off the ground. The closest I'd come to taking my fairy form to a party was the disastrous first time I'd met Nathan's family, and I'd rather get stuck in the net ten times over than go through that again.

"Good luck," Erin called after me. "Go, Blair, go!"

I flew in a loop-the-loop just to appease her, then snapped my fingers to glamour myself invisible.

This time I'll fly high enough not to get caught in a net.

What in the world had she and her boyfriend been thinking? There was no employment for an active hunter in the town, so the two of them must surely know they wouldn't be welcome among the other paranormals if word spread of her boyfriend's profession. I would have thought Nathan would have told his sister the town's unhappy recent history with the hunters at the very least. Even if she didn't know the full details… including the fact that her father had been the last person to see my mother alive.

I flew right over Nathan's head before recognising him, heading up the high street. Skidding to a halt in mid-air, I circled behind him, still invisible.

"If this was a stealth test, you'd have failed," I said over his shoulder.

Nathan almost jumped, but he caught his balance just in time. "I should have known it was you, Blair."

"Why, did the invisible glitter land on your head?" I snapped my fingers and turned visible again.

"I was sure there was someone watching me," he answered.

"Like the girlfriend you stood up yesterday?" I landed on my feet in front of him. "After explicitly promising to do better?"

He grimaced. "I was going to message you when I got back. I've just been up at the border. What are you doing here?"

"As a matter of fact, I'm looking for a net," I said. "Like the one I got caught in last night when I flew over the forest looking for a certain trespasser."

His eyes widened in shock. "You got caught in a net?"

"A rat shifter had to rescue me," I said. "I'm lucky the werewolves didn't find me hanging around, considering."

"I'd be more worried if the rogue hunter saw you," he said. "I'm sorry, Blair. I shouldn't have taken off yesterday, but I got a tip-off about a rogue near the lake and I couldn't let the werewolves find them first."

"You think it's definitely a rogue, then?" I asked, curiosity overtaking my annoyance at him.

"I think this isn't the place for this conversation." He shifted his weight. "Let's go to the coffee shop."

"Weren't you going to check for rogue hunters?"

"I just did," he answered. "Nobody's at the border except a group of disgruntled werewolves. I think it was a false alarm, or perhaps someone saw one of the merpeople on the shore. They sometimes wear clothes when they come ashore in the winter months and are easily mistaken for humans."

So Erin's boyfriend must have cleared off. I didn't want to let Nathan out of my sight now I'd found him, so I turned into my human form. Rather than opting for Charms & Caffeine, he approached the bookshop, and the cafe where we'd had our first 'date' the week I'd arrived in town.

I'd also met Vincent here for the first time, but I saw no signs of the head vampire when I scanned the shelves as we made our way to the cafe at the back. Choosing a table at a distance from the few occupied ones, I tapped the menu to order a strong coffee. Though maybe I should have picked something with a shot of courage in it instead. My stomach was backflipping at Nathan's continued silence, which continued until our drinks showed up.

"This is where we went on our first date." I picked up my mug, my hands trembling. "Does that mean this is our last one?"

Nathan choked on his coffee. "What? Of course not."

"You still haven't told me why you're being so cagey with me," I pointed out. "You could have at least sent me an update yesterday after you came back rather than leaving me hanging."

"I'm sorry, Blair," he said. "I intended to contact you when I got back, but it was so late I assumed you'd gone to sleep. I know you're under pressure at work this week, so I didn't want to wake you up."

"You could have at least asked if I'd seen the rogue." I looked down at my coffee, feeling wrong-footed. It wasn't unreasonable to expect my boyfriend to keep me in the loop, right? This was hardly different from the other murder cases we'd been involved in.

Except for one thing... his family's potential involvement.

"I know." He exhaled in a sigh. "I wasn't thinking clearly. This case... it's not good timing. We're expecting a visit from the coven next week—"

"They're inspecting the security team, too?" I raised my head. "I thought they were more interested in the covens. And Rebecca."

"The Head Witch?" he said.

"Why else would they come to town?" I said. "As your sister pointed out, it's not like we have a booming tourist industry."

A furrow appeared in his brow. "It makes sense that the local council representatives are coming to assess the Head Witch, but that doesn't explain why Steve is taking it as a personal challenge."

"He is?" I glanced at the other tables to make sure their occupants weren't listening in. "Is that why he's strong-arming you into heading this investigation?"

"No, that's because of my expertise... which he's right about," he said. "As for the inspection, I believe Steve wants to be better prepared than he was for the hunters' visit."

"Or he thinks they'll take even more authority away from him." Which meant, in all likelihood, that he'd set Nathan up to take the fall if he failed to solve the murder. *I should have known.*

"I don't doubt that," said Nathan. "He's paranoid. But I really didn't know you were in the forest yesterday, Blair. I looked for you at the border and assumed you'd left."

"Guess we missed each other." I swallowed a mouthful of coffee, which tasted like dust. For the first time in months, doubts about our relationship fluttered in my chest like a swarm of live moths. "What have you been doing all day, then?"

"Sleeping," he answered. "After I got back last night, I was awake until the early hours calling up every local branch of the hunters to find out if they misplaced any of their people. I woke up a couple of hours ago and was ordered to take a team out to patrol to the lake immediately. I'd have told you, but I didn't want to worry you with every detail, and it did turn out to be a false alarm."

"I want it. Every detail, I mean." I clenched my hands in my lap. "Anything's better than silence."

Nathan pushed back his coffee mug. His eyes were red-rimmed with tiredness. "I was afraid that if I brought you with me into the investigation, the Inquisitor would take an interest again. He'd target you, and this time, I wouldn't be able to stop him."

"Does he know?" I asked. "I mean, that one of his people might have murdered a werewolf?"

"There's little he's unaware of. He knows the coven will be inspecting the town and the new Head Witch. I can't say I know if he's heard about the investigation yet, though."

Fear welled inside me at the memory of the man even my paranormal-sensing power had shrunk away from. "He can't know, surely. He doesn't watch every hunter all the time, does he?"

"No, but most of his people are assigned to a specific area," he said. "When those three hunters conspired with Mrs Dailey and came to town, that was unusual enough that I immediately knew someone had broken the rules by inviting them here."

"What—you think someone from inside the town was responsible for the hunter coming to the border?" My stomach turned over. "It can't be Mrs Dailey this time."

She'd been hauled off to the LFPF—the same prison my dad was locked up in—for conspiring to replace Madame Grey with the hunters and her own personal group of witches. I'd done my level best to make sure she stayed behind bars, but that didn't mean the end of the hunters getting involved in Fairy Falls... and with me.

The leader of the hunters himself had extended an invitation to me to work for them, and while I'd refused, the shadow of Inquisitor Hare lurked in the back of my mind whenever I thought of the prison where my dad was locked up. It was bad enough the local witch council would be inspecting the town without the hunters' leader returning, too.

Nathan shook his head. "Most likely it's a rogue, but one who acts before thinking. Unfortunately, a lot of hunters have that trait. It's a job that draws the rash and the foolhardy."

"You don't think it was premeditated?" I said. "I mean, the guy was shot in the back while he wasn't in wolf form.

WITCH ON A MISSION

The hunter had no intention of making it look like self-defence."

"How do you know that?" he asked.

"One of the werewolves told me," I said. "If you'd messaged me, you'd know."

He winced. "I really am sorry, Blair. I hoped I could keep you out of this, but I went about it all the wrong way. I'll try to do better."

My heart twisted. "You know I forgive you, right? I just… it hurts, when you leave me hanging. But it'd hurt more if you lost your job over this case."

He exhaled in a heavy sigh. "I'll be honest, Blair, if I fail, there's little chance Steve won't demote me at the very least. My position isn't everything, but if the killer gets away with their crimes—"

"Then more hunters might take that as an invitation to overstep their boundaries against the paranormal communities." I swallowed hard. "Speaking of which, Erin admitted her hunter boyfriend wanted to move to town. Did you know?"

"Yes, but I didn't expect him to arrive until after Erin had secured a job," he said. "I told her repeatedly to think her decision through, but she's very strong-willed."

"Might it be him the werewolves spotted?" I asked. "She insists he isn't the killer, and he might not be, but the werewolves might strike the next time they see a hunter without asking questions."

"That's what I'm afraid of," he said.

"She came to see me after work," I added. "She seems to think he's sensible enough to stay away. Have you met her boyfriend before?"

"I've only met him once," he said. "But he treats Erin

well. He's certainly better than most of the hunters I know."

"Yet she thinks he can just move to town and not be ostracised by the paranormal community?" I asked. "He could be the nicest person on the planet and most paranormals wouldn't see it that way."

"I doubt he'll stay," said Nathan. "As for Erin, she'll come to her senses. If anything, she's on her way there already. She tends to dig her heels in when he's concerned."

Just as long as nobody gets hurt in the meantime.

Nathan's phone buzzed, cutting through the silence. He looked down at the screen. "I've been called to the border."

"Not again." I rubbed my eyes. "I don't want to argue with you, Nathan, but if you don't want me involved in your life—"

"I *never* said that," he said. "Never. Steve and his people are keeping a close watch on me."

"I can turn invisible," I told him. "Did you forget?"

"That didn't stop you from getting caught in a net." He went silent for a moment. "I'll text you the instant I'm home. Feel free to send your cat to harass me if I don't."

"You might regret that." A smile tugged at my mouth, but I willed it away. "I wish I felt like you had more faith in me."

He pulled me into a kiss that knocked the breath from my lungs and left my limbs quivering. "I do, Blair. When this is over, I'll make it up to you."

Breathless, I nodded. "You'd better."

He released me, and I left my unfinished coffee on the table. On the way out of the cafe, my gaze snagged on a tall pale figure standing between two rows of book-shelves, as still as a waxwork model. Vincent tilted his head as I angled towards him.

"Hey," I said, not feeling particularly well-disposed towards him after the stunt he'd pulled at the New Moon. "Recovered from your fight with the werewolves?"

"I wouldn't call it a fight," he said. "I found it refreshing exercise, actually."

I bit my lip to hold in an unwise comment—not that he couldn't read it from my mind, regardless. "I'm glad one of us enjoyed it. Do you always follow your fellow vampires into werewolf establishments?"

"No, I can't say I do," he said. "An interesting diversion, but I typically stay out of my colleagues' battles."

I think you should go back to doing that. For all our sakes. Not that I was stepping within a mile of the New Moon pub again if I could help it. It wouldn't surprise me if I'd got myself a lifetime ban along with Alissa and the two vampires.

"Oh, the werewolves know better than to ban me from their establishment," he said.

"I don't suppose your mind-reading powers have picked up on any clues as to why a hunter might have shot a werewolf at the border?" I asked.

"No," he said. "I did pick up on something about a dispute between the alpha and another family when I was at the New Moon, but I'm afraid werewolves' minds are difficult to read when they're in a frenzy. Their thoughts mostly revolved around tearing the place apart."

A dispute? Was it to do with Claude's argument with his uncle?

"I can't imagine why," I said. "You didn't need to read

minds to know the werewolves wouldn't be happy if you went into the New Moon."

There was no point in arguing with him, though. He was hundreds of years old, confident enough to know he was more than a match for a pack of werewolves.

"Were you looking for a book?" he asked. "Or perhaps an update on your cat?"

"He's still visiting you?" I didn't typically check up on how Sky spent his free time, since fairy cats were known to be inscrutable and independent. The moment I'd walked past the bookshop for the first time, Sky had picked me as his owner, and that was that.

Vincent tilted his head at me. "I gather the covens are having trouble with their newest Head Witch. A child… and you seem to have taken on the role of her mentor, too, Blair. I have to admit I didn't see that one coming."

I tensed. "Do you know—"

"Do I know the local witch council leaders will be coming here on the solstice?" he said. "Yes, I do. I also know the town has received a directive to prove that this is a fit town to host the Head Witch."

"It is," I insisted. "They picked us to host the ceremony, so it must be, right?"

"That is a matter to ask Madame Grey about, not me." He reached for the dusty bookshelf above his head and pulled down a thick volume on local history. "It seems there are many people who are displeased with the selection of an eleven-year-old as Head Witch."

"Like who?" I said. "The Rosemary witches are in jail. So are Mrs Dailey and Dr Summers."

"I cannot give you names." He skimmed the book,

tutting. "Really. They got the details of that nineteenth-century brothel completely wrong."

"Vincent—"

He looked up from the book. "I'd advise you to be prepared, Blair. Since the sceptre was claimed, the town has fallen under scrutiny. The events of the summer—the challenge to the coven's leadership, Mrs Dailey, the hunters putting us on a watchlist—have increased murmurs in certain circles that our town is a troubled element. The choice of Fairy Falls to host the Samhain ceremony was intended to soothe those rumours, but Rebecca gaining the position of Head Witch has brought out old jealousies among the region's witch council."

"I wish Rita had told me." Then I might not have got drunk at the werewolves' pub and screwed up my last lesson. "I'll do my best to prepare Rebecca, but... do you think the werewolf's death might be linked to any of this business with the council?"

"Unlikely." He slid the book back onto the shelf, an expression of disappointment on his face. "The inspection's focus is on the witches, not on the werewolves. I believe they're planning to visit certain local businesses, but they will not be travelling into the forest."

"Wait, they're coming to Dritch & Co?" Was that why Veronica was pressuring us to hit impossible targets?

"Perhaps," he said. "See you later, Blair."

He stepped behind a bookshelf and vanished from sight. I made a mental note to apologise to Madame Grey *and* Rita the next time I saw them. I could only imagine the pressure they were under, trying to get the town into the perfect condition to greet the council leaders. Not to mention Veronica, too.

As for Rebecca... I didn't dare tell her the extent of the council's inspection. She was under enough pressure already.

I left the bookshop and was halfway down the high street before I spotted Nathan coming in the opposite direction.

"They found the murder weapon," he said. "It was next to the body of another dead werewolf."

8

"They found the weapon?" I stared at Nathan. "Let me guess, you're off to look at the crime scene."

"They didn't say I couldn't bring you with me this time," he said. "I can't promise you'll be safe, but if you're certain you want to be involved…"

I wasn't, but I nodded. "Of course I'm sure."

I walked alongside Nathan, who set a pace that I could only keep up with by activating my levitating boots. In no time at all, we reached the main path into the forest, which wound between thick oak trees. I'd been in the forest countless times since my arrival in Fairy Falls and yet I remained convinced that it was designed to confuse even the most well-prepared visitor. I had only a vague sense of the boundaries between the witches' part of the forest and the less-familiar paths of the werewolves' territory to the north and the elves' lair to the west.

Glad as I was that Nathan had asked me to come with him without hesitation, my head was starting to spin.

What's wrong this time? My hangover should be long gone by now. I shivered, wrapped my hands around myself, and startled at the sight of something soft on my palms.

Fur was growing from my hands, thick and dark brown. "Uh... Nathan?"

He turned around, his eyes widening. "Blair... your face."

I raised my hands to my face. "What about it?"

"It's furry."

Oh no. "I didn't do anything, I swear. Did someone hit me with a spell?"

"Not that I saw." Nathan took my arm. "Let's head back before it gets worse."

The sound of a growl came from somewhere a few feet in front of us. "Ah, no. Will they think I'm a werewolf?"

"Quite possibly."

But judging by the volume of the noise, if we tried to leave the forest now, the werewolves would think we were fleeing the crime scene. Ahead of us lay a clearing, in which several tall figures gathered beside the body of the younger werewolf who'd been supporting Claude. Julius lay still enough that he might have been sleeping, but my paranormal sensing power remained quiet, the way it did when I was faced with someone who was no longer breathing. Inches away from his outstretched hand lay something metal and glittering. A gun.

Rustling came from the bushes behind me. I jumped when something brushed past my leg, but when I looked, there was nothing there. It must have been a small animal and not a werewolf.

"Where are they?" I whispered to Nathan. My hands

were entirely covered in fur by now. Maybe we should have turned back after all.

"It sounded like the chief was on the way to report the death when he called me." Nathan remained still, scanning the undergrowth. "The other werewolves must be close."

The bushes rustled again, revealing several were-wolves—this time, all of them in human form. Claude led the way, and his eyes narrowed when he saw me.

"Caught red-handed," said Claude. "Did you leave the weapon there so that we'd assume Julius shot himself? How stupid do you think we are?"

"Does it look like either of us has touched the weapon?" I said. "It was already here."

Another of the werewolves blinked in confusion at my hairy face and hands. "What's wrong with her?"

"An accident with a spell." Even my *voice* sounded odd, deeper than usual and slightly growly. "I've been with Nathan ever since he got the call telling him to come here, which you can verify if you talk to the chief."

"Jealous lover hexed you, did they?" said one of the other werewolves, jerking his chin at Nathan.

"Julius is dead," snapped Claude. "Show some respect. What is the hunter doing here?"

"The chief called me and told me to come at once," Nathan said. "The boy was killed by a blow to the head, not a gun. Look."

I didn't want to look, but if he'd been shot, there'd be more blood. I peered closer and saw he was right. A large fallen branch lay halfway across Julius's body, while judging by its positioning, the gun appeared to have been in the werewolf's hand when he'd fallen.

"Did you seek to throw us off track, hunter?" said Claude.

"If I was the killer, why would I leave a weapon here that I didn't use?" he said. "Check it for fingerprints and you'll find none of mine." Truth laced his words, but his brow was furrowed with worry.

One of the werewolves moved to the body and sniffed the gun. "Smells of metal and death."

"Does the scent match his?" asked Claude.

The first werewolf moved closer to Nathan, who tensed. So did I.

"No," he said. "This human hasn't handled the gun. Neither has the witch."

"We told you that." My voice came out snarlier than I'd intended. "Where is the chief?"

He couldn't be far, surely, considering he'd called Nathan and asked him to come here.

The werewolf continued to sniff around. "This one smells of the woods, like the branch that killed Julius."

"Because the branch was attached to a tree." I regretted speaking when my growly voice caused the other werewolves to bristle.

"Are you mocking me?" said Claude. "Trying to make a fool out of us?"

You're doing a spectacular job of that on your own. "No, we're here because the chief asked us to come."

"You're trespassing on a crime scene," said one of the wolves—who, now I looked closer, was one of the two who'd cornered Nathan in the clearing the last time I'd been here. I hadn't recognised him at first since he had clothes on this time. "This one even thought she'd disguise herself as a werewolf."

"Someone hexed me," I said, irritated. "Chief Donovan will confirm that Nathan and I are supposed to be here—"

"There's no need," said another, higher voice. A moment later, the rat shifter emerged from the bushes. "I saw Blair and the hunter walking here through the woods. They were nowhere near the werewolf's body *or* the fallen branch. And I saw that Blair came under the effects of the spell while she was walking. She didn't use it on herself."

Claude eyed the smaller man with distrust. "Friend of yours?"

"We don't know one another." Well, it was true. He'd helped me out of the hunters' net that one time, but that didn't make us the best of friends. "Look, just wait for the chief to show up and he'll confirm—"

Claude bared his teeth. "If the chief wasn't such a foolish, weak leader, this never would have happened."

The rat shifter shrank away into the bushes. I didn't blame him, but if Nathan and I slipped away, it might provoke the already enraged werewolves into shifting.

Then, to my relief, Chief Donovan himself appeared. "What is going on?"

"See? He's always behind the times," said Claude. "One of your people is dead. Again."

"One of *my* people?" he said. "We are all one pack, nephew. You led me to believe Julius's body was beside the border, not deep in the woods. Convenient, considering how much you complained about him hanging onto your every word. But you liked to have people follow you around offering compliments, didn't you? You always were insecure."

"What are you saying?" said Claude.

Whoa. I held my breath when several more werewolves

97

emerged from the woods behind the chief, forming a circle around the clearing.

Chief Donovan stepped over to the gun and knelt to examine it. "This is not the murder weapon. Someone planted it here in an effort to convince us to blame the hunters, rather than someone closer to home."

Claude growled. "You mean to say you believe one of your own werewolves did this?"

"I don't believe the killer was human." He gestured at the fallen branch. "Few could have knocked over a tree without assistance."

"The hunters could," Claude insisted. "They'll shoot us all in our beds if you have your way. Already they're inviting themselves onto our territory without permission."

"I invited Nathan here myself." Chief Donovan bared his teeth. "If you have a problem with how I run things, then I'd suggest joining another pack."

Time to go. The werewolves didn't need us here, and they also seemed to have forgotten about the hunters in lieu of blaming one another. I took a half-step towards Nathan, and a chorus of growls broke out among the group.

"You've flaunted the rules for the last time," Claude told his chief. "I've had enough of you giving everyone orders."

"You seem to ignore the rules when it suits you," said Chief Donovan. "You're as weak as your father."

Claude's face began to turn hairy. "You only enforce the rules because it's an excuse to pander to the witches and beg them for more territory rather than winning it fair and square."

Nathan took my arm, and we backed into the bushes. I prepared to snap my fingers and glamour us both invisible, but one of Claude's friends spotted me first. "Thought you'd sneak off, did you?"

"You're just jealous because she looks more like a werewolf than you do," said one of the chief's allies. "You look like a half-plucked chicken."

A flush heated my face. Great. I was hairier than the werewolves, apparently.

Then a flash of light drew everyone's attention to the undergrowth behind us. A tall figure dressed in grey strode into the clearing, her silvery hair shining in the light of her glowing wand.

Madame Grey studied the werewolves, wearing the look she usually reserved for misbehaving students. "That's quite enough," she said. "If I may remind you, we have a meeting of all the paranormal communities this weekend and if you decide to challenge your uncle, Claude, there won't be time for a new leader to fill out the necessary paperwork before the event. Assuming you leave each other in one piece, that is."

The werewolves gaped at her, stunned into silence for what might be the first time in their lives. I hadn't thought the witches had any influence over who was chosen as pack leader. Then again, when it came to leadership, the covens worked with all the other paranormal communities, and if another werewolf took power at a critical time, the outcome had the potential to affect the whole town. A critical time like right before a major inspection from the local council, for instance.

"You have no authority here—" began Claude.

"You voted for my authority to override yours when

you agreed for the pack to be part of Fairy Falls," she said. "And you ought to do well to remember the reason you had to sign the agreement is because you and certain other wolves insisted on walking naked through town at inappropriate times."

I stifled an unexpected laugh. At least they'd stopped snapping at one another, though now their ire seemed to be directed at Madame Grey instead. I hardly believed she'd actually strode right into the middle of their territory. Then again, if she thought the werewolves' arguments had the potential to affect the outcome of the inspection, who could blame her?

I leaned closer to Nathan. "I didn't know Madame Grey could interfere in pack matters without being eaten alive."

"The pack respects her leadership over the town," he said. "For now, at least. Also, I suspect someone from within the pack called her like they did me. Otherwise, she'd have been challenged."

Not only were the witches under scrutiny, but it looked like the council would be coming here to an unsolved set of killings. And on top of that, if I didn't figure out how to undo this spell, I'd have to greet them looking like I was dressed in a furred suit.

How do I always end up in these situations?

———

Nina gave me an appraising look. "I can either use a shaving charm or a hair-loss spell. But that would cause *all* your hair to fall out. Eyebrows, eyelashes, the lot."

Our neighbour was a hairdresser, so she had the

expertise on my situation. Tall and curvy with long hair, Nina lived in the flat above ours and gave us free haircuts whenever she got bored. I sat on the sofa and tried not to scratch too much, though my new hair itched like crazy.

"No thanks." I shuddered. "I'd rather keep the moustache."

"You do look very dashing." Alissa stifled a grin.

I scowled. "I can't go into work with my hands like this. How am I supposed to use a computer? Or the telephone?"

"You went into work while transparent once, didn't you?" said Alissa. "Just explain to your colleagues and it'll be fine. Then it'll be the weekend."

I lifted my furred hands. "And what if it can't be fixed?"

"All spells can be fixed," said Alissa. "It's not a curse, at any rate."

"I'm not so sure it was a spell either," I said. "Are there potions for rapid hair growth?"

"Possibly," said Nina. "Did you annoy anyone recently?"

"No," I replied. "I mean, I did annoy some werewolves, but they thought I was making fun when I showed up on their territory like this."

"I can't believe you went there." Alissa rose from the armchair, her wand out. "Even when Bryan and I were together, he never took me to meet his family in the forest. We always met at the New Moon pub."

"I doubt either of us is welcome *there* now." I tried to scratch my face, but a thick coating of hair got in the way. "Thanks to a certain vampire. Why can't you date normal guys?"

At least her boyfriend wasn't giving her the silent

treatment, a voice in the back of my head said. *Don't start, Blair. Nathan's under a lot of pressure, and he's promised to do better.* The fact that he hadn't laughed at my furry hands and face was proof enough he was a keeper.

"Miaow," said Sky.

"Sounds like he agrees with me."

Alissa prodded me in the spine with her wand. "Samuel said he's very sorry the werewolves trashed their own pub. He'd have apologised directly to them, but he has himself a lifetime ban from the New Moon. Which is a literal lifetime, to a vampire."

I snorted. "Has he told you how old he is yet?"

Alissa suddenly became very interested in examining my furred hands. "Mm."

"That wasn't an answer," I said. "He's hardly as old as Vincent, right?"

"Nobody's as old as Vincent," said Nina. "Except maybe the wandwood trees."

She wasn't wrong. The elder vampire was the town's oldest resident at over eight hundred years of age. Samuel wasn't that old, but there was still an age gap between him and Alissa that she'd avoided discussing in depth.

Alissa drew in a breath. "He's young for a vampire."

"Younger than Edward Cullen?"

Nina choked on a laugh. "Please at least say he hasn't been celibate the whole time."

Alissa's face went brick red. "Don't be ridiculous. He's less than two hundred, though."

"Practically a teenager." I hoped Alissa knew what she was doing. She came across as calm and level-headed, but she had a wild streak that came out occasionally, and a well-known case of terrible judgement when it came to guys.

"That explains why he started a bar fight with a wolf pack," said Nina. "Blair, I can use a localised hair loss spell until you find a more permanent solution to reversing the spell if you like."

"Only if you promise not to scalp me," I said. "Or make my eyebrows disappear."

"I'll do my best," said Nina. "Keep still…"

Nina waved her wand. At once, the hair vanished from my hands, and the relentless itching on my face died down a little.

"Hey, it worked!" I turned my palms over, relieved to see human skin in the place of fur.

"It's not permanent," she added. "If the spell turns out to last longer than a few hours, you'll have to learn to reapply it yourself. But you can use a slow-growth spell to stop it growing back as fast."

"All right." I pulled out my wand.

"Don't point that thing near me," said Alissa. "I'd like to keep all my hair, thanks."

"Miaow," said Sky, in tones that suggested if I made one strand of his fur disappear, *he'd* pull what was left of my hair out.

Work was going to be fun tomorrow.

———

"Blair, what's wrong with your face?" said Bethan as I entered the office wearing a hooded coat and a balaclava.

As Nina had warned, the spell's effects had begun to return after a few hours. While the slow-growth spell had brought it under control, the odds of me getting through the day without walking out looking like Sasquatch were slim.

I'd assumed the cold weather would be a good excuse to hide the lower half of my face for as long as the moustache and beard persisted, but I should have guessed my co-workers would see through it. At least it was Friday, which meant two upcoming days free of clients and targets. I'd just need to avoid scheduling any face-to-face interviews before Monday.

"Nothing," I said, my voice muffled. "Think I'm getting flu."

"Well, don't give it to me," said Lizzie. "I have to spend tomorrow helping my sister install the new coffee machine at the cafe."

"Good luck with that." I coughed, trying to sound congested and not growly.

I'd expected Veronica to comment on my new attire, but she merely peeked into the room to make sure we were on task, before retreating to her own office and locking the door. Rob and Callie were absent again, which left me with nobody to ask about how last night had ended. I doubted the werewolves would appreciate me telling the whole office that half the wolf pack suspected one of their own people of using a hunter's weapon to murder someone, while the other half feared an outsider was trying to pick them off. Nor that Madame Grey had had to intervene, either. She must be concerned about the local council's visit. Who could blame her, when it looked like the hunters and the pack were at odds at the worst possible time? Not to mention the pack itself seemed on the brink of erupting into a full-blown conflict.

Meanwhile, I remained in the dark as to who had put the hair-growth spell on me. By the end of the workday, I still looked presentable enough to be seen in public, so I headed to the witches' headquarters even though I didn't have a lesson today. Rita wasn't in the classroom, but Madame Grey answered when I knocked on her office door.

"Blair," she said. "I thought I'd be seeing you today."

I was that predictable? "Is it okay if I speak to you?"

"Of course. Close the door and come in."

I did so, and she looked me up and down. "Did you drink a hair-growth potion?"

"Not sure," I said. "It was either a spell or a potion, but I can't say I know who did it."

Blythe? She'd lurked around the coffee shop when I'd first moved to town and hexed me so that I'd fall on my face in front of Nathan, so she was the obvious choice of suspect, but I'd thought she wasn't able to use hostile spells against me any longer. I *had* seen her the other day, and I couldn't think of anyone else who'd find it amusing to give me an extra coating of hair.

"Is there a way to undo it?" I asked.

"I expect it'll wear off on its own, but I'm afraid we don't have any hair-loss potions in stock," she said. "That isn't what you wished to speak to me about, is it? You wanted to know how I came to find out about the confrontation between the werewolf pack members."

"Did the chief call and tell you to come?" I'd worked that much out.

"He did," she said. "The other werewolves might not all be fond of reporting their actions to the covens, but it's that or send a team directly into the forest myself for regular assessments. In any case, I saw it as my duty to intervene before the werewolves faced any more casualties."

"I didn't know," I said. "That you knew about werewolf pack matters, I mean."

"There's little I don't know about inner workings of this town, Blair," she said. "If another wolf issues a challenge to his leadership, Chief Donovan will be obligated to prove himself. However, if the challenger is humiliated and defeated, he'll be driven out of the pack, so it's only chosen as a last resort when the challenger is confident that he can win."

I turned this over in my mind. "By challenge, do you mean they'll fight one another? Claude would fight his own uncle?"

"Yes, he would," she said. "I can only hope that they wait until *after* this murder case is dealt with, for all our sakes."

"I agree," I said. "Do you think one of them was the killer, though? The werewolves? Because Chief Donovan himself seems to think so."

He couldn't suspect his own nephew, right?

"I disagree with him," she said. "Given the presence of the gun, it's clear there are hunters near the border who shouldn't be, but until we identify them, we can't make any assumptions."

I opened my mouth to speak and then closed it. Did she know Nathan and his sister might know who the trespasser was, if not the murderer?

"In any case, Steve is examining the weapon right now and he should be able to work out where it came from," she said. "That's all the information I have, Blair."

"And… the council inspection?

Her lips pursed. "Rebecca has guessed, hasn't she?"

"It's next week," I pointed out. "If I were her, I'd want to know."

"She's a talented witch," she said. "If the council saw what she can do with her talent, they'd have no doubts that she is worthy of the title of Head Witch."

"Do you know where she is right now?" I asked.

"She's in the empty classroom, practising," she said. "She's been here almost every day in her spare time between lessons."

"She didn't tell me that."

"Would she?" said Madame Grey. "She already feels behind her peers. She doesn't want you feeling she's holding you back."

Wait, was she worried about disappointing *me?* Did she put me into the same category as the other adult witch authority figures, including Rita and Madame Grey? *Of course she does.* I mean, she was eleven. It might be weird to think of anyone considering me an expert on magic, given my history, but it was only natural that Rebecca wouldn't see things that way.

"Okay. I'll talk to her."

I left her office and headed to the classroom. When I opened the door, Rebecca jumped, dropping the sceptre. The plastic box she was levitating fell to the floor.

"Sorry!"

"No harm done." I smiled. "You were doing just fine then. I just startled you."

"Mm." She looked down. "I can't do it when anyone else is around."

"Is that the issue?" I said. "Want me to give you a

private lesson over the weekend? Not with Rita. And not at the witches' place if you don't want to. We can pick a spot somewhere and practise those spells with nobody watching."

"Uh, sure," she said. "I'm busy tomorrow, but I can do first thing in the morning on Sunday. Blair, why are your hands so fluffy?"

Oh, no.

9

On Sunday morning, I woke to a flash of glitter and opened my eyes to see a little winged figure flitting about above my head. The pixie. "Hey there," I croaked. "Long time, no see."

The pixie resembled a stick insect-sized miniature figure with wings and pointed ears. After he'd stolen the sceptre from inside my room, I'd somewhat lost my trust in him and he probably sensed it, because it had been weeks since he'd visited.

I woke up a little more. "Hey… has my dad asked you to deliver a message? Is he coming to meet me on the solstice?"

Please say yes. The paranormal prisons forbade visitors, but the solstices were important days for fairies and my dad claimed that he was allowed to leave the jail for that one day. No doubt he'd be surrounded by guards, but I'd take any conditions as long as it meant I got to see him.

The pixie dropped a note on the bed. I scrambled to pick it up and found that fur covered both sides of my hands again. *Oh, no.* Nina had reapplied the hair loss spell, but it must have grown back overnight.

I grabbed the note, which read, *Blair, I heard about the inspection coming to Fairy Falls. Be careful. I promise I will send you another note when I find out the best way to communicate.*

That was it. He couldn't have forgotten the solstice was next week, could he? What did he mean by 'the best way to communicate'? Weren't anonymous letters delivered via pixie safe enough for him?

I grabbed a notebook and pen to scribble out a response. "He must know I have a million questions I can only ask him in person," I told the pixie. "Like how he wound up locked up in jail to begin with."

I'd worked some of it out. If the hunters hadn't killed my mother, then the fairies had been involved somehow, however little sense it made. I mean, my dad *was* a fairy. But when I'd spoken to my mother's ghost, she'd told me not to trust the fairies at all.

Granted, it looked like I'd be spending most of the solstice avoiding the inspecting council members instead. Over the last few weeks, Dad's notes had been so brief and unhelpful that I'd hardly felt like I had a father at all. Not that I didn't have enough to worry about, what with the werewolf murders, the inspection, work, and whoever had decided to curse me with hair growth, but was it too much to ask that my one surviving blood parent make the effort to come and see me?

Sky stuck a paw out from under the bedcovers and swiped at the pixie, causing him to fly out of reach.

"Hey!" I leaned back as Sky clawed his way onto the

bed and took another swipe at the little fairy. "Sky, quit that."

The pixie flew out of reach of Sky's claws and disappeared in a flash of purple glitter.

"Thanks a bunch." I grabbed my half-written note and got to my feet.

The fur had spread halfway down my arms and all over my face, but Nina already knew about my predicament and nobody would be in the garden at this hour in the morning. Grabbing my slippers, I ran out of my bedroom, through the living room, and out of the flat into the hallway. I found Sky sitting in front of the doorway to the back garden, as though he'd walked through the wall. Which he probably had. It wouldn't be the first time.

"What's the matter with you today?" I scanned the garden, but the pixie might have glamoured himself invisible for all I knew. "All right, since I'm awake, can you teach me how to walk through walls?"

"Miaow." Sky licked a paw. I took that to mean, 'nah'.

"Or can you teach me how to glamour all this extra hair invisible?" I went on.

Sky moved on to cleaning his other front paw, totally indifferent to my plight. Then he turned away and padded back into the house. Maybe I wasn't advanced enough at fairy magic to learn that trick, or he wasn't interested in teaching me. It was too cold to hang around outside looking for the pixie, so I returned to my flat before anyone spotted my furry features.

I found Alissa in the living room, removing her coat. A long scarf was wrapped around her neck.

"What's up, Blair?" asked Alissa. "Went for an early morning walk?"

I closed the door behind me. "Did you just get back?"

"Late shift, remember?"

I thought it finished four hours ago. Her face was very pink, and she made no move to take off her long scarf.

"What's with the scarf?" I asked.

"It's cold."

"Not in here." Our flat was practically toasty, especially with the extra hair all over my hands. "You don't need to hide anything from me, right? I know you were with your vampire boyfriend. Did you tell him not to follow you into any more werewolf establishments?"

"I did," she said. "He didn't mean things to escalate the way they did. He was just concerned we'd get caught up in a pack dispute."

"Guess he read it from someone's mind." I rubbed my furry face. "I'm going to need Nina to redo the hair-vanishing spell."

She grinned. "Yeah. I mean, don't get me wrong, I think you rock the half-wolf look, but the werewolves might take offence."

"They did. It's lucky Madame Grey showed up when she did."

"Yeah, that's weird," she said. "I've never heard of her getting directly involved in pack business before. I know she's supposed to be in charge of everyone in town, but who wants to see a naked elderly wolf doing his business in the river?"

"They've never been shot at by hunters in their own forest before, have they?" I said. "Also, thanks for that mental image."

"You're welcome." She sat down on the sofa, and Roald

crawled out from under a cushion onto her lap. "What did you end up doing yesterday, then?"

"Sleeping. Studying. Contemplating my many mistakes." It'd been rainy and miserable for most of the weekend, and with only a few short days until the inspection, the best I could do was avoid running into any more drama before then. "Nathan was working on the case, but in the office. Taking the gun apart, he said."

"Any new conclusions?" she asked.

"The gun was empty." I went to put some food out for the cats. The instant I opened the cupboard, Sky appeared. At least some things were predictable.

"And the victim wasn't shot," she said. "A branch fell on him, right? So did someone plant the gun at the scene to frame the hunters?"

"The gun was close enough to his hand that he might have found and picked it up before the branch fell," I distributed the cat food between the two bowls and went to the kitchen to wash my hands. "Since nobody witnessed the attack, all they've been doing is arguing about it. I'd have gone to the police station yesterday, but apparently, the werewolves were giving Steve grief all day."

"Isn't Nathan meant to be in charge of the case?" she said.

"Not according to the werewolves. Except for the chief and his allies, but I wouldn't be welcome getting involved as long as I look like this." I waved my paw-like hands.

"Did you ever find out who did that to you?" Her gaze went to my face. "Your moustache is coming back, too."

I groaned. "I have no idea who did it. They must have hit me somewhere between the cafe and the forest.

Vincent was in the bookshop at the time, so maybe he saw."

"I can ask Samuel to speak to him," said Alissa.

"Only if he doesn't declare war on whoever did it. I've had quite enough drama this week." I flopped onto the sofa. "On top of that, the pixie showed up in my bedroom when I woke up, and Sky scared him off before I could figure out if my dad remembered next week's the solstice or not."

Her hand paused mid-stroke. "You're meeting your dad?"

"I don't know. He hasn't said." I reached to stroke Roald, and Sky popped up instead, shoving his way onto my lap. "He just wanted to warn me about the inspection, as though I don't already know."

"How does he know?" she asked. "I guess that pixie tells him everything."

"That, or the hunters are keeping tabs on us. Which would be just my luck." I stroked Sky, who rolled onto his back, batting at my face. "Yes, I know I have hair in places I'd prefer not to."

Sky made a coughing noise that might have been a laugh.

"Very funny," I said. "Madame Grey herself said it'd go away on its own, so it must be a long-lasting one. I'm doing my best, but I don't want to try a hair-removing hex in case it blasts off my eyebrows."

"Madame Grey said that?" Alissa's brow furrowed. "I can check with Samuel if he has a book on cures for hair-growth potions and spells, if you like."

"I'd rather not have anyone else find out if I can help it." My phone buzzed. Reaching for it, I checked my messages and saw Nathan's name. At least he'd kept his word about updating me even when there was nothing going on, but…

Am at the police station with Erin. Weapon wasn't used for murder.

"What's up, Blair?" asked Alissa.

"They figured out the gun Julius was holding wasn't the murder weapon," I said. "But it sounds like Erin is at the police station with Nathan. I guess they hauled her in for questioning."

So much for not showing my hairy face in public. I got to my feet, narrowly avoiding dislodging Sky, who followed me into my bedroom, meowing indignantly. I pulled on my clothes at lightning speed, gave Sky an apologetic stroke, and was halfway out the flat before I realised I'd forgotten my shoes. I backtracked, grabbed my boots and shoved them on, and broke into a sprint. I regretted not wearing a coat by the time I stumbled, breathless, to the doors to the police station. Even my extra layer of fur didn't keep out the chill.

Nathan walked out of the doors and started when he saw me. "Blair, what are you doing here?"

I clutched a stitch in my side, wheezing. "You implied it was urgent."

"You aren't going to be allowed into the questioning." He gave me a concerned look. "Is that spell still in effect? I thought your friend used a counter-spell."

"The hair grew back overnight." I peered over his shoulder, but nobody aside from Clare was in the lobby. "Is your sister being questioned now?"

"She is," he said. "She turned herself in so her boyfriend wouldn't get caught. I warned her not to, but

Erin refused to listen. I'm not allowed into the questioning, since I'm related to her."

"Was her boyfriend definitely the hunter who was spotted near the border?" I asked, dropping my voice.

"I don't know," he said. "The police conducted a thorough examination of the weapon and concluded that it likely wasn't used in the second murder. There were no bullets inside it."

"But there might have been if it was used in the first murder, right?" I said. "Is there a way to tell?"

"Unfortunately not," he replied. "That said, no traces of any hunters have been found in the forest, so we've yet to figure out how the weapon got there."

"Does the chief still think it was planted there on purpose?"

"He does. It's not making him very popular." He glanced over his shoulder. "Steve's attention, however, is now focused on Erin."

"Why'd she turn herself in? Because of the sightings at the border?" She'd already known about them the last time we'd spoken, so that couldn't be right.

"No." He paused. "It was because I made the mistake of mentioning to her that the weapon is one that belongs to our family."

My throat went dry. "It does? How would you know?"

"There's an emblem on the side," he said. "Not something a non-hunter would know, but the crest indicates it belongs to our branch of the hunters. If it's not someone in my family's, then it's someone who works for them. Erin decided it wasn't worth the risk of me taking the fall, so she went to speak to them herself."

My chest went tight. "Does Steve know?"

"He's not knowledgeable enough about the hunters' crests to identify it, and I didn't tell him," he said. "Don't panic, Blair. My family owns that entire hunters' branch and I don't believe any of them committed the murder. As long as Erin doesn't let anything slip—and she won't—he'll let her walk out free. She's trying to ensure neither of us takes the blame."

My phone buzzed. I checked the sender's name—Rebecca. I'd totally forgotten the extra lesson I'd promised her this morning. "I have to run, Nathan. I promised to give Rebecca some tutoring—you know, the new Head Witch. But seriously, if they suspect your family—"

"They don't," he said. "Erin knows what she's doing."

I wasn't so sure, but the last thing I needed was another argument with Steve. If I admitted I'd been trying to help Erin find employment, he'd drag *me* into her questioning, and it wasn't fair to skip out on Rebecca's lesson with the inspection a mere few days away.

"I'll text you later," I said. "I have to get the hair loss spell redone before my lesson if I don't want Rebecca to think *I'm* one of the werewolves."

"I can talk to Steve when the questioning's over," he said. "Tell him someone hexed you."

"Please don't," I said. "It doesn't exactly make me look any more credible, does it? No wonder the police think I'm a laughing stock."

"You aren't." He gave me a hug. "We'll sort this, Blair. Including the hair growth."

"I'm surprised you don't mind being seen with me," I mumbled into his shoulder. "I guess after the wings, nothing's a surprise."

"You aren't wrong, but I'd never be ashamed of being

seen with you." He brushed a kiss to my forehead and released me. "Never."

―――――

After begging Nina to top up the hair loss spell, I hurried to the witches' headquarters and found Rebecca waiting in the lobby.

"Sorry I'm late," I said.

Rebecca blinked at me. "Why are you wearing your shirt inside out?"

Knew I forgot something. "I had an early start. But I'm ready for our lesson."

I needed the distraction, even if it involved being turned into an ornament or dyed pink—both of which had happened during our recent lessons.

"Okay." She glanced at the open classroom door, gripping the sceptre as though recalling how it'd burned a hole in the wall. "Are we staying in here?"

"Where do you want to go?" I asked. "There are empty classrooms. Or the lawn around the back, but it's not the best place for privacy. I had my first flying lesson there and ended up being laughed at by a bunch of kids *and* their parents."

"You got laughed at?" Her surprise threw me off. Surely if she'd witnessed any of my screw-ups during our lessons, she'd know I was as far from an expert witch as it was possible to be. Or even the more recent incidents, like the accidental hair growth. In fairness, I wasn't actually responsible for that one, but despite all that, she really did think of me as one of the adults. I'd spent so many years feeling out of place that it hadn't occurred to me that Rebecca would naturally see me as someone who had her life together even when it certainly wasn't the case.

"You should have seen me try to mount a broom for the first time," I said. "I had to get my cat to sit on the end because my wings kept getting in the way."

She laughed. "Really?"

"Of course. You could teach me a thing or two," I said. "You're more persistent than I am. Anyway, I'll just grab some props, and we'll find an empty field somewhere."

She brightened. "Okay."

"Not too close to the lake," I added, heading into the classroom. I opened the cupboard and fetched a box of the props Rita used in her classes. "That way, there won't be anyone watching."

"I can't do my exam with nobody watching," she mumbled as we left the witches' headquarters. "The entire council will be there on Wednesday."

"Did Rita tell you, then?"

"Madame Grey did," she said. "She asked me to talk to her yesterday. I know the local council leaders are coming to inspect the whole town. Rita's put all this time into training me and I keep screwing up."

"Have you met the council members before?" I asked.

"I've never met their leader, Angela. I'm afraid she'll be mean, like my mother," she said quietly.

"You don't know that for certain," I said. "Madame Grey wouldn't let you go ahead with the test if she was certain the council would try to fail you."

"They're coming to town because of me to begin with," she said.

"Not because of you alone," I said. "Your assessment

will only be a small part of the inspection, and it won't cover anything you don't already know how to do."

"It doesn't matter if I know to do it." Her voice trembled. "I can pass my exams with a wand, but to qualify as Head Witch, I need to do it all over again with the sceptre, and if I screw up, they'll take it off me. I don't want to go through all this and then let everyone down."

I understood. Part of her didn't *want* to hold the sceptre, since she hated the attention, but if she failed the test and lost her Head Witch title, her classmates would go right back to bullying her again. The sceptre was a shield against them, not to mention losing it publicly would be a huge blow to her already fragile confidence.

"You were really good at the levitating spell when you didn't know I was watching you," I said encouragingly. "Perhaps you can pretend nobody is watching during the test, too."

"That won't work," she insisted. "I won't be able to forget when I'm standing in front of an audience."

"Then pretend they're a glamour," I suggested. "Fairy glamours can make anything look real. They can even turn someone invisible."

"You can do that," she said. "Right?"

"I can." I snapped my fingers and turned invisible. "Tell you what, I'll stay like this while you practise the spells. Does it make it easier for you to pretend I'm not here?"

"A little, but it's weird hearing you talking to me when I can't see you." She walked ahead of me down the road, while I snapped myself visible and invisible a few more times.

We veered off the path and walked into the hills until

we reached a clear spot. The grass was slightly damp from the frost, but out of sight of the lake.

I laid down the box of props. "Which do you want to try first?"

"Levitating," she said.

After picking out one of the plastic bricks from the box, I snapped my fingers and turned invisible. "Like I said—pretend I'm not here."

"I can still hear your voice." Rebecca held up the sceptre, and I remained quiet, flitting in mid-air.

After a moment, she raised the sceptre and performed a perfect levitation spell. Then with another wave, she returned the prop to the ground.

"See, you can do it." I turned visible, then invisible again. "Try again."

"Okay." Her tone became more enthusiastic. She repeated the spell three more times, each successfully.

Then I snapped my fingers and turned visible in the middle of her waving the sceptre, and the levitating spell hit the box instead. Everything inside it flew into the air and scattered all over the grass.

"Oh no!" she said.

I waved my own wand and flipped the box the right way up. "You did just fine. Tell you what, now you can try to levitate everything back into the box."

With a snap of my fingers, I turned invisible. This time when I appeared mid-spell, she didn't falter. The brick flew back into the box she'd aimed it at.

"There, you did it this time," I said. "What changed?"

"It's okay if I look at the sceptre," she mumbled. "And if I don't look at whoever is watching me."

"Then do that in the exam," I said. "There's no rule

against it. Besides, you need to be looking at the sceptre if you want it to work."

"Rita always tells me to look at the target instead."

"That might work when you're using a wand," I acknowledged, "but the sceptre is much bigger than you're used to, and harder to control."

"But they might ask me to levitate a bigger target," she said. "Like a person."

"Nah, the health and safety risks would be too high even with a wand," I said. "But if you'd like to try, feel free to practise levitating me. I can use my wings to fly back to earth if you lift me too far."

Her expression cleared. "Okay."

With a wave of the sceptre, I went airborne. Her spell lifted me above the ground, and I used my wings to flutter back to earth.

When it seemed she'd grown confident enough in the levitation spell, I returned the props to the box and moved onto the next spell. Two hours later, she helped put the props away in a positively cheery mood.

"I wish you were allowed to come into the exam," she said.

"I can ask," I said. "But I'm not really qualified as an examiner. Just remember everything we practised, and you'll be fine."

We parted at the lesson's end with both of us feeling more confident in Rebecca's chances of passing the exam. While Rebecca went home, I headed to the witches' headquarters to return the props and found Blythe waiting outside the classroom.

"You have hair on your nose," she said, by way of a greeting.

"Thanks." I closed the classroom door. "Was it you who hexed me in the bookshop? Because your timing might have been better."

"What?" She blinked. "I'm still under the binding spell. I haven't set foot in there in months, besides."

I turned to face her. "Why are you here, then? Your sister already went home."

"Why else?" she said. "You're encouraging my sister to actually go through with this ridiculous exam? Half the adult witches in town couldn't handle it."

"I'm trying to help her," I said. "And she's doing a great job, actually. I think she's in with a shot. So do Rita and Madame Grey."

"They're wrong," she said. "She could be as good as it's possible to be with that sceptre and it'll make no difference. The council will take it off her, our town will be a laughing stock, and we'll be wide open for—"

"For what?" I said. "What do you think is going to happen? Is it to do with your mother?"

She made a strangled noise, then shook her head. "It doesn't matter."

"That doesn't sound like nothing," I insisted. "Come on, at least tell me what I should be prepared for."

"I thought you already knew," she said.

The hunters? Not the fairies, surely—she knew less than I did about them, after all. Then again, her mother and mine hadn't got along. There was some history there, and I had an inkling it went beyond the little I'd found out during my time in Fairy Falls.

Blythe merely shook her head and walked away. As she did so, my phone buzzed with a message from Alissa telling me that Samuel had got in touch and was going to meet us at the coffee shop with some information on reversing hair-growth spells and hexes.

With his mind-reading skills, perhaps he could find the culprit, too. If not Blythe, who had enough of a grudge to put a spell on me?

10

I met Alissa at Charms & Caffeine. As before, she wore a thick winter coat and a long scarf, hovering outside with her hands wrapped around a paper cup of something warm and delicious-smelling. "Samuel's inside. How'd it go with Nathan and his sister?"

"Erin's being questioned, but Nathan hasn't texted me with an update yet. I had to run off and give Rebecca some training practise, so I'm waiting for him to text me."

I walked with her into the coffee shop. Samuel sat at a table, sipping a mug of what I strongly suspected was blood. At least this cafe had a menu that catered to vampires, so he hadn't had to bring in his own supplies, like he had at the werewolves' pub.

Alissa startled at the sight of him. "He wasn't here when I went outside. He must have slipped in while I wasn't paying attention."

"Vampires." *Honestly.* "Did he at least say he could help me deal with this curse?"

Samuel looked up. "Hello, Blair," he said. "You have some admirable facial hair."

"Thanks." I wasn't feeling particularly warm towards him after his stunt at the vampires' pub, despite Alissa's insistence that he'd been trying to act in her best interests. I mean, the girl was smitten.

"The menus aren't working today," said Alissa. "They're installing a new coffee machine, so they're making everything by hand."

Right—Lizzie had mentioned she'd be helping her sister over the weekend. Pulling up my jacket to hide the lower part of my face, I went to the counter to speak to Layla.

"Hey, Blair," she said. "Is that vampire with you? I haven't seen him before."

"He works at the university," I said. "I guess he doesn't leave the library much, but he's dating Alissa."

"The same Alissa who brought that vampire apprentice here a while ago?" she said. "I think your friend might have a thing for vampires, Blair."

"You aren't wrong." I spotted Lizzie fiddling with the coffee machine and a possibility occurred to me. "Can I have a coffee? And can I ask you a question?"

"Sure," she said. "You're not after another lucky latte, are you?"

"Probably shouldn't risk it." The coffee shop's infamous lucky lattes might give a good luck boost, but they also came with a backlash that lasted weeks, and I'd had quite enough bad luck without adding to it.

Layla turned her back to make the coffee. "Or a hangover cure for werewolf cocktails?"

"No." Even she'd heard about that? "I wondered—do you know the staff who work at the bookshop cafe?"

"I do," she said over her shoulder. "Why?"

"I fell under some kind of hair-growth spell while I was in there," I explained. "I wondered if someone spiked my drink with a potion."

Layla waved her wand over the coffee cup in a complicated motion. "We normally make the drinks ourselves and send them straight to the table, and the staff at the bookshop café do the same. So unless someone sneakily used a spell while the barista's back was turned, I don't see how they could have done it."

Lizzie popped up behind the counter. "Hey, Blair. What did you do to your face?"

"Not sure yet," I said. "Do either of you know a potion that can cause facial hair growth? I think someone might have spiked my coffee the other day, because I would have noticed if they'd used a spell."

"I can check." Layla turned around and handed me my drink, and I fumbled to find some cash to pay for it. "In the meantime, you might want to look up antidotes."

"Thanks." I picked up my coffee and walked back to the table to join Alissa and Samuel.

"What were you three chatting about?" asked Alissa.

"This." I indicated my half-hidden face. "I think the person who did it might have spiked my drink at the bookshop café. It's the only time I can think of where I wasn't paying attention."

"You'd have tasted it, surely," said Alissa. "Growth potions are strong."

"My coffee was strong, too." I sat down opposite her.

"It's been two days, and the effects haven't shown any signs of stopping."

"If it's anything like normal potions of that nature, it will stop after a few days, provided it isn't reapplied." Samuel gave the coffee cup in my hand a pointed look.

I shrugged and took a sip. No hair-growth potion was going to come between me and my caffeine fix. "That means it'll be gone before the solstice, right?"

Samuel took a sip of his drink. "Some particularly potent doses can last a month or longer."

…or maybe not. "A *month?* I can't interview clients like this."

"Sure you can." Alissa winked. "You can pretend to be the office's pet yeti if you apply enough white hair dye. Didn't you have a client who was looking for someone to hire to pull sledges?"

"Ha ha." I ducked my head over my coffee, my face heating under the coating of fur. "I suppose dyeing it would be easier than making it disappear."

"I think white hair would suit you," said the vampire.

I decided not to dignify that with a reply. "Have you seen Vincent lately?"

"Any particular reason?" said Samuel.

"He was in the bookshop when the hair-growth spell was put on me," I said. "He's observant, so he might have seen who did it."

"I doubt it," he said. "I imagine he'd have told you if he had."

"Depends if he'd have found it as funny as everyone else does." I drained the rest of my coffee. "I'm going to head to the library to look up an antidote. Preferably one that won't make the rest of my hair fall out."

"That would be unfortunate." Samuel rose to his feet, and in the blink of an eye, he was gone.

"Doesn't he even say goodbye?" I said to Alissa.

"He's a vampire. They usually don't bother with pleasantries." Alissa picked up what was left of her coffee. "C'mon, we can walk up to campus. He'll have found a dozen books by the time we get there."

Okay, there were *some* upsides to having a best friend who was dating a vampire librarian. Like access to the town's best store of magical handbooks, for instance. I wished he'd been able to find out the culprit. If Blythe and the werewolves weren't responsible, I was at a loss to figure out who else I'd annoyed lately. Maybe a potion with mildly irritating effects was enough to get around the spell preventing Blythe from doing me harm, but she'd seemed genuinely confused at my accusation. If the person who'd done it meant me harm, they could have done a lot worse than turn me into a werewolf. The potion was pretty tame, all things considered.

Alissa and I walked uphill through town, shivering in the cold air. The town's university campus was decked out for the holidays, the dragons and griffins on the murals dressed in Santa hats and the poplar trees covered in glittering lights. Fake snow fell from artificial clouds someone had levitated over campus, while shimmering tinsel adorned every windowsill. A life-sized model of Santa and his sleigh occupied one side of campus, except with unicorns instead of reindeer. Students lobbed snowballs at one another or skied down artificial slopes set up between lecture halls. Rubbing my hands together to keep them warm, I opened the library door to toasty warmth and a roaring fire in the grate.

Dozens of towering shelves filled most of the space, arranged in circling patterns that seemed designed to confuse anyone who didn't have a vampire's rapid walking pace and sense of direction. I squeezed past a group of students levitating baubles onto a tree, while Dr Appleton's assistant, Vera, rambled about her research thesis to anyone who would listen. For once I was glad of the extra hair, because it stopped her recognising me. With my long coat and hairy face, the pupils probably thought I was a bearded professor, which at least made a welcome change from being mistaken for a student.

Samuel popped up, a book in his hand. "I found your antidote. There's a potion you can brew in an hour that reverses cosmetic effects like hair growth."

"Perfect," said Alissa. "We can brew it later, right, Blair?"

"Sure." By the look on her face, she was hoping to spend more time with Samuel, and I was not in the mood to play third wheel. "Thanks, Samuel. If you hear from Vincent, can you let me know?"

Resigning myself to another day resembling a wookiee, I left the library and walked out onto the campus. The fence surrounding the place reminded me I wasn't far from the town's border. Ducking a snowball hurled by an overenthusiastic weresquirrel, I moved closer to the fence, my gaze snagging on the DO NOT CLIMB sign.

Had anyone from the university seen the hunters trespassing near the border? It was worth a look around, since I was here. With a snap of my fingers, I turned invisible and flew up so I could properly see over the fence at the back of campus. The dark mass of the forest was a short distance away, while a blond figure dressed in black walked down the path. At first, I thought he was a were-wolf, but his muddy boots and hiking gear made my heart give an unpleasant swoop. If the clothing wasn't enough of a clue, I could tell by the way he walked that he was a hunter.

Think, Blair. I held my breath when he neared the trees, but then he walked right past the forest and paced along the border of the campus, apparently oblivious to the hundreds of paranormals on the other side. He continued to pace, giving the occasional scan of his surroundings as though looking for someone. He wasn't openly carrying any weapons, but then again, Nathan didn't either.

Was he Erin's boyfriend? She ought to know better than to risk him being arrested, but maybe she didn't know he was here. Perhaps he'd heard she was being questioned by the police and had come to meet her.

I flew over the border, snapping my fingers to turn off the invisibility. The hunter jumped in astonishment. "Whoa. Where did you come from?"

Up close, his hair was more pale gold than blond, while his dark clothes were tough and durable. His fine-boned face and blue eyes were striking enough that I understood why Erin had the hots for him, but he also looked oddly familiar in a way I couldn't place. Perhaps it was just that he wore the same hunter-style clothes as Nathan and his siblings did.

"You're Erin's boyfriend," I said.

"I'm Buck," he said. "Who are you?"

"Blair Wilkes," I said.

He looked over my shoulder, then at the ground. "Did you just appear from thin air? Is that glitter yours?"

"Maybe." I'd hoped to sound mysterious and interesting, but the purple sparkles on my shoes were a dead giveaway. Also, I'd forgotten to put my wings away.

"What's with the hair?" he added. "Are you a werewolf? Because I've never seen one with wings."

"Never mind." No wonder he looked so confused. What with the wings and the fur combined, I looked nothing like any other paranormal creature in existence. "You might not know, but two recent murders took place not far from here, and the main suspects are the hunters. Why are you pacing around here in broad daylight?"

"I don't want any trouble," he said. "I'm just here to see Erin."

"Last I heard she was being questioned by the police about said murders," I said. "Does Nathan know you're here?"

"Who... oh, Erin's brother. I don't see why he wouldn't. He comes this way often enough."

Huh? Nathan had implied Buck had left town, but if he planned to move here, it made sense that he'd set up a base close by while Erin was staying in town.

"You're less than a mile from a forest inhabited by werewolves and elves and a lake filled with sirens and merpeople," I said. "That campus contains a few thousand paranormals, too. You're lucky nobody jumped you."

"I have a few tricks up my sleeve," he said.

"Does that include the gun we found in the woods?"

He blinked. "You found... wait, you *found* my gun? I wondered where that went."

I stared at him for an instant. The gun was his? Had he used it to shoot—okay, I was way out of my depth here. I had zero authority to make arrests, but if there were more of his fellow hunters on their way to town, I didn't want to be responsible for bringing them here without first telling Nathan or the police.

"The gun is being held as evidence in a murder case," I told him. "The same murder case your girlfriend is suspected of being involved in. How exactly did it end up in the forest?"

His mouth parted. "The forest? I haven't been near there."

True. My lie-sensing power was faultless, however absurd his claims might be. So had someone stolen it from him, or had he shot the werewolf from a distance? Then what about the second victim, killed by a falling branch, who'd shown up with the gun next to his hand? None of this added up.

He tensed. "Someone's coming."

I turned around, spotting Nathan at the foot of the hill. Relief swept over me. "Hang on. I know him. He's…" I trailed off.

Buck was gone. *How did he move that fast?* Maybe hunters had something of the paranormal in them after all.

Nathan looked up and saw me. "Blair, is that you?"

"No, I'm a fairy werewolf," I said. "I was on my way to brew up a cure for this spell, except I just ran into a certain murder suspect."

I pointed in the direction where Buck had vanished. *How did he disappear so fast?*

Nathan blinked. "Who?"

"Erin's boyfriend, of course." I folded my arms across my chest. "You *knew* he was coming here, didn't you?"

"I assumed he'd have more sense." Nathan shook his

ELLE ADAMS

head. "I should have guessed that he'd have drawn his own conclusions from Erin's arrest."

"He doesn't seem to have much sense of self-preservation," I said. "He also said the gun was *his,* but someone stole it and planted it at the crime scene. And according to my lie-sensing power, he was telling the truth. What is even going on here?"

His expression darkened. "If it's true... then the police need to be informed. Erin won't like it, but it'll prove that neither of us was the weapon's owner."

"Someone *did* shoot the first victim." Which made even less sense now, unless we had two killers on the loose. "What if Steve doesn't think it's enough proof? We only have our word, and mine isn't worth much to him. He could just jump to the conclusion that Buck dropped his weapon in the forest while he was running away. It's not like any of the werewolves have actually seen him in there."

Nathan's mouth pressed together. "No... but they *have* seen him at the border. Turning him in will quell the rumours of there being a rogue on the loose. As for the murders—"

"How can we turn him in if he's vanished?" I scanned the field beyond the campus, but I saw no signs of the hunter's presence at all. "Since when could hunters move using vampire speed? I could have sworn he went that way, but I have no idea where he's staying."

"The nearest town is within walking distance," Nathan said. "I can ask Steve to call and ask if he's staying there. Erin won't be pleased, but either she lets herself get locked up or she brings Buck in for a trial. I'm sure she'll pick the latter."

"Then I'm going home to fix my hair before someone on the university campus starts a rumour that Sasquatch is camping near town." I shook my head. "I wish I could do something for your sister. I'm not convinced Buck turning himself in will convince Steve to let her go."

"No... you're right. We need more proof." He turned to the woods. "That fairy trap you flew into might work. If you bring that to the police, it'll prove Erin wasn't involved. They discontinued those nets years ago."

"Except that means a different hunter was in the forest," I said. "Question is, who?"

Nathan's gaze panned across the thick oak trees. "I wish I knew."

11

F inding the fairy trap took less time than I'd expected, thanks to Nathan's knowledge of the forest's many winding paths. The remnants of the sticky web remained suspended between the trees, and when I tried to pull it loose, my fur-covered hands became entangled in a skein of webbing.

"This was a mistake." I tugged against the webs, grimacing when they caught in the hair on my palms. "Webs and hair-growth potions don't mix. How do the hunters even manage to free the people they catch in these?"

"That's why they were discontinued from use. The hunters were as likely to get caught in the nets as their targets." Nathan gave a gentle tug and succeeded in freeing one of my hands, only for me to stumble back and get my feet tangled as well.

A yelp came from elsewhere in the bushes, and I jumped. "I don't think we're alone here."

Nathan stiffened. "That doesn't sound like a werewolf."

"Get me out of here!" yelled a shrill voice.

I kicked my feet free of the webbing and found one of the elf king's assistants, Bramble, lying sprawled in the half-collapsed net.

He blinked up at me. "Blair? What curse are you under? Have you turned into one of the children of the moon?"

"No, I'm under a hair-growing spell." At this rate, I'd never live it down. "Don't move. I'll get you out of there."

With Nathan holding one end and me the other, we managed to unravel the net until the elf was able to wriggle free. Most of it ended up stuck to my furred hands in the process, which, as it turned out, *hurt* when they were pulled out. Gritting my teeth, I yanked the last of the sticky threads away from the elf, who landed on his feet without so much as a thank you.

"Evil sniffs at our borders," he said matter-of-factly.

"You mean the werewolves?" I asked.

"The solstice is next week," he continued as though I hadn't spoken.

"I know." What I *didn't* know was whether, after six months of waiting, I would get to see my dad, or if the universe would yank the carpet out from underneath me yet again. "You celebrate the solstice, too?"

"We do, but we will be staying underground this year," he growled. "Evil masks its features and we will not let it into our homes."

I brushed my hands on my coat in an attempt to remove the remaining strands of webbing. "Do you mean the fairies? Do you still think they're coming back?"

He'd given me a warning to that effect a while ago, but I'd seen no evidence of any fairies aside from myself and the pixie.

"Coming back?" he echoed. "They're already here."

"You mean *me?*" I said. "Did you see who put this net here?"

"No," he said. "I was walking along the path, minding my own business, when I became ensnared."

With a great deal of dignity, he removed the last strands of webbing from his sleeve and walked away into the undergrowth.

I shook my head at Nathan. "Honestly. Sometimes I think the elves and the vampires consult one another to decide how best to be maddeningly cryptic."

"I doubt it." Nathan reached into his jacket and pulled out a pocketknife. "Let me cut that off you."

The knife easily sliced through the last bits of the webbing, and I brushed it off my palms. "I'm going to brew up the cure for the hair-growth potion as soon as I'm home. This has gone on for too long."

"Are you sure it's wise to brew up the cure yourself?" he asked. "Not that I'm questioning your abilities…"

"But you did witness that time I turned myself transparent," I finished. "Yeah, that's why I was waiting for Alissa to finish seeing her fanged friend first. In the meantime, let's get this trap together and take it to the police."

It took another half-hour, and liberal use of Nathan's pocketknife, to remove the remainder of the sticky trap and transfer it into a sack Nathan produced from his coat pocket. He lifted the sack over his shoulder and walked ahead, while I hurried along, checking my phone every so often. No messages from Alissa. *Guess I'm going to the police station disguised as a wolf, then.*

When we reached the police station, it was to find the place swarming with gargoyles, including Steve himself. He glanced in my direction and tutted. "No werewolves in here."

"I'm not a werewolf," I said, flushing beneath all the hair. "It was a mistake."

He studied me more closely. "Blair Wilkes? Did you get bitten by a wolf?"

"No, I'm under a spell."

"If you've come to report it, take it up with Frederick here." He indicated the gargoyle I'd dubbed Ink Face after an incident involving the office printer, who smirked at the sight of me covered in hair. Great.

"That's not why I'm here," I said. "I came here because someone set up a trap in the forest near the werewolves' territory using a net designed to ensnare shifters."

"This," said Nathan, holding up the net. "It's an old type of net that was discontinued by the hunters. Someone hung it up in the forest, which backs up our theory that there's someone else near town who shouldn't be there."

"You think that will *help* your sister's case?" said Steve. "She might have left it there herself. I told you not to meddle, Nathan, and I also gave you explicit orders not to bring your girlfriend into it."

"I didn't fly into the net on purpose," I said. *He ordered Nathan not to bring me into the case?* "We had to rescue an elf who got caught in it, too. Doesn't the idea of someone leaving traps for paranormals in the forest worry you?"

He ignored me. "I have had about enough of your

family members, Nathan. Your sister spent the afternoon plying me with ridiculous excuses as to her presence in town."

"Can I question her?" I asked. "I can verify if she's telling the truth or not."

"There's no need," he said. "She's been released as a suspect. Nathan, leave the net here, and do tell me anything else you might have neglected to tell me about your wayward family members and their friends. Any others staying in town that you decided not to mention?"

No way. He can't be accusing Nathan.

"There's no need for that," said Nathan, with a glance at me. "I can take it from here, Blair."

I opened my mouth to argue, but Ink Face moved in. "Thought you were going to chop off your hair," he said, with a sneer.

He herded me towards the door and out into the street, and I resigned myself to a solo potion-brewing session.

When I got home, I found Erin on my doorstep. She crouched beside Sky, stroking him while he purred contentedly.

"How'd you know where I lived?" I stopped in front of the unlikely pairing.

"Nathan," she answered. "He wasn't at home, so I thought he'd be with you."

"He's at the police station now," I told her. "I heard they released you as a suspect. Want to come in?"

I hadn't figured out how to persuade her to get Buck to talk to the police and stop them from pinning the blame on Nathan, but given his disappearing act earlier, I had an inkling it wouldn't be easy.

"Oh, sure." She straightened upright to let me unlock the door, and she and Sky followed me into the corridor. When I opened the door to my flat, she gave the living room an appreciative scan. "Nice place. You live with... Alissa, right? Madame Grey's granddaughter."

"Yeah." I closed the door behind me. "I was going to brew up a potion, if that's okay with you. The cure for this." I raised my furred hands.

"I thought you were keeping them," she said. "Extra hair is convenient in this weather. The hunters could learn a lesson or two from you."

I reached into my bag, pulled out the potion book Samuel had given me, and made my way over to the kitchen cupboard where Alissa and I kept our stores of potion ingredients. "Want some tea?"

"That'd be great." She sat down on the sofa and Sky made himself at home in her lap. "I was joking, don't worry. I haven't talked to the hunters. So my brother's back with the police? What did they have to say about your new look?"

"They thought I was a werewolf," I muttered, feeling my face heat up. "Steve's concerned that Nathan might be hiding his knowledge of other hunters in town, since he didn't tell the police you were here."

Erin looked up from petting Sky. "First I've heard."

"Are you sure?" I turned around as the kettle finished boiling, and I finished making the tea. Erin was silent until I walked over to join her on the sofa.

"That Steve guy is as thick as a plank," Erin said.

I put down the cups on the coffee table. "I could say the same of your boyfriend."

Her face fell. "You saw him."

141

"He was wandering around by the university campus," I said. "You know how many witches and wizards live on the other side of that fence who could permanently turn him into a turnip for trespassing?"

"I told him not to." She blew on her tea to cool it. "He was probably just worried about me."

"The gun was his," I told her. "He claimed someone stole it and planted it in the forest."

She lowered her cup. "Maybe someone wanted to frame him."

"Who, a werewolf?" I said. "Does he personally know any of them who might have a grudge against him?"

"No." She leaned back as Sky stretched in her lap, demanding attention.

"Then who?" I pressed. "Another hunter?"

She shrugged, putting her teacup down to give Sky another stroke. "Maybe. I don't know, I haven't seen him since I arrived in town."

"Where is he staying, then?" I asked. "He vanished into thin air as soon as I turned my back."

"In the next town over," she said. "I already messaged him when the police let me go to explain I was off the hook, but he has more sense than to cross the town's border. Did you have all that hair when you spoke to him? No wonder he ran off."

"Don't remind me." I rolled my eyes. "I think he thought I was a fairy wolf. Or a bearded wizard. You know, like the ones from *Lord of the Rings.*"

Erin choked on her tea. "Nah, you look more like one of the dwarves."

"I'm not *that* short. I met an elf today, and they're about four feet tall."

"You met an elf?"

"That's how Nathan and I ended up at the police station." I explained how we'd retrieved the net and taken it to Steve and the others. "And let me tell you, those nets are a nightmare to handle with all this hair. I can see why the hunters stopped using them."

"You aren't wrong," she said. "So who put the net there in the first place?"

"That's what Nathan wanted to know," I said. "I don't have any idea who they were trying to catch. Not a fairy, since there's only one of me."

"I keep forgetting that," she said. "I mean, fairies are rare in the paranormal world, but I forgot you were the only one living here."

"Definitely the only one with paws." I retrieved the book with the antidote and headed for the potion cupboards again. "I'm going to brew up the cure. Wish me luck."

"Ooh, you're doing magic? Let me see." She bounded to her feet, to Sky's annoyance, and tailed me to the kitchen.

I laid the library book down on the work surface, starting to regret my decision to invite her to watch. "It's not really magic. I mean, it's not like waving a wand and summoning pretty lights."

"Or glitter." She grinned. "Or pixies, elves, and that cat of yours. You know, he was sitting on the doorstep when I got here like he was waiting for me."

"Imagine that." I opened the cupboard and started pulling out ingredients. "He doesn't like it when you stop petting him."

Sky meowed loudly behind her, and she went to give

him some attention. Roald emerged from Alissa's room to greet our guest, and the two cats kept Erin occupied while I sorted the ingredients into piles.

"I didn't get the job I interviewed for, by the way," she told me. "I'm sorry about the trouble. Buck had no idea there'd been a murder when he came to meet me. I should have guessed my brother would end up heading the investigation and get himself into trouble. He's always been the noble sacrificing sort. That's why it didn't suit him, being one of the hunters. We're trained to look out for ourselves alone. I think it suits him better being here. Being with you."

I kept my eyes on the ingredients to avoid meeting her eyes. "I feel like he always considers my safety before he considers what I want."

"That sounds familiar," she said sympathetically. "Nathan was free to sign up to the hunters all he liked, but as soon as I tried to do the same, he got big brother syndrome and tried to intervene. He can't seem to help himself."

"Mm." I read and reread the first line of ingredients then tossed the cut-up leaves I'd prepared into the cauldron. "I'd mind less if he didn't keep running off alone. What about Buck, then? He's still an active hunter, but if he's still going to move to town, that might cause trouble."

"He plans to hand in his notice, but it doesn't make sense for both of us to quit at once with no employment waiting for us here in Fairy Falls," she said. "Also, the Inquisitor is away at the moment. Not sure where. Maybe he's taken a holiday."

"He is?" I tried to picture the Inquisitor lounging on a

beach, but my imagination failed me. "What about your dad?"

"He's at home, same as ever," she said. "And he's still mad at me for leaving the hunters. He can hold a grudge like nobody else I know. No wonder my mum has no time for him. I lived with her after she split with my dad and I only went back to join my brothers when I decided I wanted to sign up to the hunters. Mum's a witch, but she prefers living as a normal. I think she'd like you."

So that was why Erin wasn't as devoted to the cause as her older brothers were, with the exception of Nathan.

"I'd like to meet her someday," I said.

"What about your—oh, right, your dad's in jail, right?" She paused. "So who raised you?"

"My foster parents are great," I said. "They're also normals, and they retired a year ago to go adventuring in Australia. They don't know anything about the paranormal world, or anything that's happened since I moved to Fairy Falls."

She let out a low whistle. "Wow, that's going to be a bit of a shock, right?"

"I'm not *telling* them." I tipped a handful of powder into the pan. "I can't. The law forbids it, and I'm not about to get on Madame Grey's bad side."

Erin moved closer to watch me stir the potion. "I haven't met her yet. Madame Grey, I mean."

"She doesn't normally introduce herself to everyone new in town unless they plan to join one of the local covens," I explained. "She took an interest in me because I'm the first new witch in years to move to town without knowing my magical heritage. And it's only got more complicated since then."

"No kidding," she said. "So your dad's a fairy? I gathered as much, but Nathan won't tell me why he's in jail."

"That's because he doesn't know, and neither do I."

As I carried on brewing the potion, I found myself telling her all about being half-fairy, about the shock of learning my dad was in jail—and even, in a low voice, I admitted that her father had told me my mother had died on the run and he'd been the last person to see her alive.

When I'd finished the last part, Erin had gone uncharacteristically quiet. "I didn't know... I swear I didn't know. My dad didn't say a word to me about your family."

"I didn't expect him to," I said. "Nathan had no idea. I guess your dad must have told his supervisors and that's it. Nobody here in Fairy Falls even knew my mother was dead, since she left town years before I was born."

"I'm sorry," she said. "I wish they allowed visits to the jail, but I guess if they did, the serial killers would take advantage."

"They don't allow visits?" I stopped in the middle of stirring the potion. "But I thought—I mean, I heard the fairies were allowed to leave the jail on the solstice, with supervision."

"Not unless they changed the rules recently," she said. "Though now I think about it, they did give the rulebook an upgrade just before I left. Something about closing the gaps in the visit schedule. No exceptions."

They'd changed the rules? Why hadn't my dad told me? "I heard that my dad and the other fairies were allowed supervised visits on the solstice back in June."

"If he's not allowed contact with you, he won't have been able to tell you," she said, in sympathetic tones.

I opened my mouth and closed it. I might have

146

admitted some of my secrets, but I hadn't mentioned the pixie, or my correspondence with my father. It wasn't my secret alone, even though I trusted Erin, and the very last thing I wanted was to lose my last tenuous connection with my dad.

But what if I'd already had?

12

I woke up the following morning covered in fur. Thick strands lay all over the bed, the floor, and even clung to the walls. I sat up, brushing my hands, and the fur came away. The potion had worked—but the fur hadn't vanished. Instead, it'd fallen off overnight, and given my restless sleeping habits, the whole room was covered. Including...

"Miaow," said Sky, from beneath a nest of hair.

The upside: the cure had worked. The downside was that I now looked like I'd taken a nap in a weresquirrel's nest. I went to the shower, shedding fur everywhere, and took a long scrubbing session to get myself free of hair. On an ordinary day, I'd be more annoyed, but my mind was elsewhere.

My dad wasn't going to be able to see me on Wednesday, and he hadn't even *told* me. Not only that, morning brought no more new messages from Nathan, and now I knew how closely Steve was watching him, I couldn't even blame the guy. It was almost a relief to know I had to go into work and deal with whatever troublesome clients the day threw at me, just to have something to distract me.

Once I'd cleared up most of the hair by using cleaning spells that left Sky sulking about the loss of his nest—as it turned out, he liked building fortresses out of hair almost as much as he enjoyed destroying my bubble wrap collection—I went off to work.

"Oh, good, you're back," Rob said, when I entered the office. "I was starting to think you'd got yourself bitten by a rogue werewolf. I was going to invite you to join the pack."

"Not quite." I sat down, brushing yet more fur off my clothes as I did so. "Someone pranked me with a potion, I think."

"The steady-growth draught?"

I frowned. "Should I know it?"

"It's a werewolf potion used on cubs who can't perform a full shift," he explained. "It works because it has no taste."

"No taste? Really?" I was starting to think the werewolves had a potion for every occasion. If it was true, no wonder I hadn't tasted it. Granted, I hadn't been paying close attention at the time, and I'd ordered an extra-strong coffee, after all.

Bethan and Lizzie entered the office before I could ask if a werewolf might have had reason to use the potion on me. To dissuade me from investigating the murders, perhaps. I'd have asked Rob or Callie if the pack was aware of Buck's presence near the town, but that would send the rumour mill spinning even more than it already was. I'd just have to hang tight until Nathan got in touch.

To add to my frustration, the clients seemed to be on a mission to be extra annoying today. I finally hung up on the shop manager who wanted to catch twelve unicorns to pull Santa's sleigh and refused to listen to my protests that there were no qualified unicorn-handlers free on Christmas Eve.

"Maybe we should have just let him do it himself," Bethan said. "What's next?"

I checked the next client on the list, who wanted to hire five 'Mind-Wipers' for a wizards' fireworks display on New Year's Eve. "What's a Mind-Wiper?"

"Someone who erases the memories of normals who witness magical shenanigans," said Bethan. "Sightings of magic always triple around this time of year, especially during New Year celebrations. Mostly the normals in question are too drunk to remember, but a lot of witches and wizards forget themselves and make a public spectacle."

"I can imagine," I said. "So I'm basically looking for people who want to supervise and won't mind not taking part in the festivities?"

Shockingly, there were few volunteers. I hung up on the twentieth person in a fit of despair as the office door blew open.

"How are you getting along?" Veronica swooped into the office, a tinsel scarf draped around her neck. "No… this won't do at all."

"What won't do?" said Bethan. "Unless we all cast ten cloning spells, we'll never get all this done by the new year."

I looked up. "I know about the inspectors from the

local witch council. But they aren't coming here, are they?"

"The inspectors?" Rob's brow furrowed in confusion.

"The collective of local witches in charge of assessing the Head Witch... and her home," said Veronica. "They will be arriving in town on the solstice, and assessing every business in town, including ours. If they see the absolute chaos that takes place in this office on a daily basis, nobody in their right minds will ever hire us again."

"Chaos?" echoed Bethan. "You mean the clients? They're responsible for ninety percent of it, at least."

"This is no laughing matter," said Veronica. "In the last few months, we've had murders, ghosts in the office, the business with the personality-altering spell, a printer attacking a police officer—"

"The inspectors don't know about any of that, do they?" I said.

"No," she admitted. "However, Angela Eagleton is a former colleague of mine, and we once belonged to the same coven. She's the sort of person who can sniff out trouble anywhere, and our clients are nothing *but* trouble."

"That's hardly our fault," said Bethan. "Besides, we got an influx of new clients after you were cleared of murder, and even more after the ghost showed up. Not that it was ideal, but it put our business on the map. Besides, it's not a formal inspection, is it? You own the place."

"I do, but Angela has the authority to pass judgement on whether we're allowed to continue operating as we do."

My mouth fell open. "They can shut us down, just like that? Why didn't you say so before?"

"I didn't want to distract you from your tasks." She sighed. "Angela has made no secret of her opinion that setting up a paranormal recruitment office was a waste of time. She's looking for an excuse to fail us."

"Then we'll prove it isn't," I said. "Don't forget students get turned into toads at the academy on a regular basis. The inspectors aren't going to shut them down, are they?"

Veronica still looked doubtful, so Bethan added, "Frankly, I think she'd be relieved if we told her about all the troublesome clients we've dealt with over the years. Wouldn't anyone rather we took the troublemakers off their hands?"

"Exactly," said Lizzie. "I'll get the coffee machine to brew up special drinks for the inspection and ask the printer to print out a welcome poster."

"I'll tidy the office," said Rob. "We'll come up with a plan to distract them from asking unwanted questions."

With our new mission in mind, we returned to work with added enthusiasm. I forgot all about my disaster of a life as I helped the others tidy the place up and come up with a game plan to deal with the upcoming inspection. We even cleaned the printer, which contributed by loudly singing *Jingle Bells* at everyone who got too close.

"It actually has a pleasant singing voice," said Rob. "Maybe it could duet with that goblin opera singer."

"Blair?" Veronica paused beside my desk. "You have permission to leave work early."

"Early?" I frowned. "Why?"

"Steve has requested that you come to the police station to attend Nathan's trial."

13

Nathan's trial. He hadn't been working… he really *had* been arrested as a suspect.

I'd been in the trial room more often than your average citizen, but this was the first time in a while that I'd been there as a witness. More than a few of the gargoyles gave me suspicious looks as I entered, taking a seat on the opposite side from the big chair covered in chains which sat at the centre of the main interrogation room. The grim-looking chair was currently unoccupied. Nathan wasn't here yet.

How had he gone from being head investigator in this case to a suspect? It had to be Steve's doing. He blamed Nathan for not telling him about Erin, true, but perhaps his annoyance at Nathan taking over his security team had caused him to finally crack. He'd been itching to get Nathan for something ever since he'd more or less stolen the police's credibility from underneath him, but it was Steve's own fault for letting standards slip to begin with.

The rest of the gargoyles filed into the room, filling the

seats which formed a circle around the throne-like central chair. I held my breath as the final two gargoyles entered, flanking Nathan himself. It was all I could do not to jump out of my seat and stop them from putting him in that chair. Or offer to take his place. Which, I suspected, was exactly what he'd done for his sister and me.

Maybe it wasn't Nathan being an overprotective numbskull, but that he'd go out of his way for the people he loved. Right now, I wanted to give him an adoring thwack on the back of the head for taking the fall. Or shout 'I love you' across the courtroom.

I really was an idiot. How had it taken me this long to realise?

Erin entered the room, wearing an expression as stony as the gargoyles', and took one of the unoccupied seats. Then two blond werewolves entered: Chief Donovan and Rob.

I watched them walk in, startled. Were they here to defend Nathan… or help pass judgement on him? It was hardly fair, given the animosity between the pack and the hunters, but Steve wasn't known for his diplomacy. The werewolves didn't speak a word, just took their seats among the other spectators.

Once the room was full, Steve took centre stage, his wings spreading from his shoulders. He'd taken on his gargoyle form, probably so he looked more intimidating than usual.

"Let us begin," he said. "This man has been accused of committing two murders. Or covering up those murders and assisting the murderer."

Steve did not excel at making speeches. It was all I could do not to roll my eyes as he listed Nathan's supposed crimes, including neglecting to mention two fellow hunters were staying in or near town.

"A hunter killed two werewolves recently," Steve went on. "Or at least someone with access to one of their weapons. Nathan is a respected member of our town's security team, yet he is both a former hunter and someone who is prepared to lie to protect his former colleagues."

Anger blazed within me as the chains on the central chair closed in around Nathan, and I bit down on the inside of my cheek to avoid shouting at Steve. *He's innocent.*

"Who wouldn't lie to protect their family?" Erin burst out. "Besides, it's not against the law for people who worked for the hunters to come to town for any reason."

"He lied about the presence of killers!" Steve snapped. "I heard from multiple sources that the hunter called Buck is staying in the area—"

"I told you that myself," said Nathan. "I also told you I had no reason to suspect him of being guilty."

"Then why was his weapon in the forest?" Steve glared at him.

"Because someone planted it there," said Chief Donovan. "I believe Nathan is innocent of all crimes."

I couldn't have been more surprised if he'd pulled out a tutu, put it on and started dancing a jig.

"You do?" Steve looked equally surprised at the pack chief's declaration.

"Yes," he said. "He came to the pack's territory at my own request and has repeatedly helped to defend my pack as well as the town as a whole. We've had our differences, but he has done nothing to suggest he would turn against anyone from our pack. In addition to that, Blair Wilkes can sense truth from lies, and she verified that he speaks the truth. While he may have deceived you, neither he nor Buck is the murderer you're looking for."

I could have hugged the werewolf on the spot. *Thanks, Chief.*

Steve shook his head. "The weapon found on the scene belonged to your family. Do you deny it, Nathan?"

"No," he said, "but my father runs the local hunter branch. I've never hidden that fact. Since he supplies all the weapons and marks them, I would be surprised to find a hunter's weapon anywhere in this region which didn't carry his mark. It doesn't mean I personally was involved, nor any of my family members. Furthermore, as I verified myself, the weapon wasn't used to commit the second crime and there's no proof it was involved in the first. If you'd like to speak to Buck, I'm sure he'd be willing to answer questions about how his gun came to be taken into the forest."

"Then who shot the first victim?" said Ink Face. "The gun picked itself up and hid itself in the forest, did it?"

"Don't be absurd," said Nathan. "You've searched my property enough times to verify that I don't own any weapons like that one."

"You might have hidden it elsewhere," Steve insisted. "I made you head of the case and you repaid me by making a mockery of us."

"Nobody's mocking you," said Erin. "If people think you're a fool, it's your own doing."

Steve's face turned alarmingly red for a grey-skinned gargoyle. "I have had enough of your family overstepping your boundaries—"

"If I may intervene," said Chief Donovan. "Two of my people were murdered, and you've yet to conjure up a single accusation which isn't connected to your own ridiculous feuds. I'd like to request that you put your jealousy aside and apply yourself to investigating the murder of my pack members."

"Jealousy?" Steve's face turned purple. "I am not jealous of those honourless hunters. I gave Nathan a chance to bring in the culprits, and he failed every time. Why should I trust his word?"

"There's a simpler way." Vincent walked in. "I can verify everything Blair confirms."

All eyes turned to the leading vampire, who strode to the centre of the room, his suit impeccable and his eyes glittering with amusement.

"Well, Blair?" he went on. "Can you ask the accused to confirm his innocence?"

What is he playing at? The vampire's presence had silenced Steve, for a wonder, so I turned to Nathan and said, "Did you commit either murder, Nathan?"

"I did not."

"And Erin?" I went on, at Vincent's prompting.

"I didn't murder either of those pack members," said Erin in a clear voice. "And to my knowledge, neither did Buck."

Vincent nodded to Steve. "That man is innocent. So is his sister. Also, if you were wondering who was responsible for stealing the office's supply of iced buns, you might want to ask Frederick."

Ink Face spluttered, but Steve growled, "This is preposterous. In two days' time, the local council's inspec-

157

tors will arrive in town. At this rate, they'll arrive to an unsolved slew of murders."

I knew it was about them.

"I doubt they'd be thrilled to find you locked up an innocent man either," said Vincent. "Haven't you learned your lesson from the last time?"

"Are you challenging my authority?"

"Do you deny my powers?" Vincent gave him a smile with a deliberate flash of his fangs.

"No…" The gargoyle faltered. "No, I do not."

The pack chief climbed to his feet, his attention on the vampires' leader. "Vincent, kindly enlighten me: do you believe another pack member is responsible for these killings?"

"I do not believe anyone in this room is responsible," he said. "But I cannot say I know if your pack is involved. As I recall, they were somewhat distracted when I went to speak to them at the New Moon."

"And is there any reason you decided to intervene?" said Steve. "You told me you'd never come to give evidence in a trial again."

"I came here as a favour to a friend," said Vincent.

Who? Me, or Nathan? With Vincent, it was impossible to tell. Maybe Samuel had asked him to come. I didn't know, but none of that mattered now Nathan was free.

Steve bared his teeth. "Fine. Nathan is cleared of all charges, as is his sister. Gargoyles, return to the office, and if I see one iced bun out of place, the person responsible will be cleaning the prison's lavatories for the next week."

All the tension whooshed out of my body. The chains on the chair withdrew, freeing Nathan, and everyone rose to their feet and made for the door. There'd been more people in the interrogation room than I'd thought. Were-wolves, weresquirrels, even the odd rat shifter or two.

As we escaped into the street, I threw my arms so tightly around Nathan that he let out a surprised *oof*. "Blair, I can't breathe."

I released him. "I'm so glad you're cleared."

"Things looked pretty rough there for a moment," he said.

"I'm glad Vincent showed up," I said. "And Chief Donovan spoke for you. To be honest, I'm not sure which surprised me more."

"The pack chief keeps his word," he said. "I *am* surprised about the vampire, though."

"You and me both," I said. "He doesn't typically get—"

"Involved?" Vincent finished. "The quicker this case is cleared up, the better. There's something else you wanted to ask me, isn't there?"

I rotated on the spot to face him. "Something I wanted to ask?" Wait a moment. "Did you see anyone in the book-shop's cafe when I was there with Nathan? I think someone spiked my drink with a hair-growth potion. I already used an antidote, but I wondered if you might have seen who did it."

"You do?" His brows rose. "No... I didn't see anyone."

Guess it was worth a try.

"Blair." Erin hurried over to us. "I'm going to—you know, meet someone."

She means Buck. I wanted to tell her to berate him for Nathan's sake, but not with Vincent standing there. The vampire eyed her with interest, but he didn't offer a comment. Considering he must be reading her mind, he surely knew her secrets, but I never could predict what the elder vampire would do next. With a short nod, he vanished with a vampire's swift speed.

"I don't understand that guy," I said. "Or vampires in general, come to that."

"I wonder why he felt the need to intervene," said Nathan. "He seems to be doing it more and more frequently lately."

"Perhaps he's annoyed that the police still aren't taking my lie-sensing power seriously," I said in an undertone. "Or perhaps he really was concerned about those iced buns. Does he owe *you* a favour?"

"He didn't say." He took my arm. "Come on. We have time enough to chat about this later, but I think we should make the most of our freedom."

No kidding. I couldn't stop grinning, despite the lingering spectre of the unsolved murders. Nathan was no longer a suspect, and Vincent had actually helped out for once, seemingly for reasons irrelevant to his own interests. It was a miracle. If not for the upcoming visit from the council with the murders still unsolved, I'd have skipped through the street.

"Steve's really worried about the inspection, then," I said. "He's not the only one. My boss is, too."

I told him about my eventful morning at work as we walked down the high street, safe in the knowledge that neither of us was going to get locked up as a murder suspect.

When we reached the end of the street, I spotted a decent-sized crowd gathering outside the witches' headquarters. Strange. It was the middle of the day, and I'd thought half the town was at Nathan's trial.

"What's happening over there?" Nathan asked.

"Very good question." I picked up the pace, drawing closer to the group. Spotting Rita among them, I made a beeline for her.

She looked up and saw me. "Blair. Rebecca is missing."

My heart dived. "Isn't she supposed to be at school?"

"She never showed up this morning," said Rita. "Mrs Farringdon says she hasn't seen her since last night."

"She was under a lot of pressure," said another witch. "Perhaps she ran away."

"Is the sceptre missing, too?" Dread curled around my heart like a viper. The timing was too suspicious. She hadn't run. She'd been taken.

14

Nathan's concerned gaze met mine. "Blair, are you sure she didn't run away? You said she was worried about being tested at the inspection, right? Perhaps she wanted to be alone for a while."

"Even if she went off by herself, she's still at risk."

Not just from the killer, whoever, it was, but from anyone who had reason to be interested in gaining power over the new Head Witch. Rita had warned her not to go anywhere alone, but perhaps Nathan was right, and she'd gone out wanting to get some peace before the testing began. I wanted to believe that, but Rebecca ought to know better than to take the sceptre away from the witches' headquarters.

"I agree," said Rita. "Anyone with an interest in manipulating the Head Witch has been watching out for this moment. We have to find her, and fast."

"I'll tell the police." I turned back the way we'd come. "Steve won't be thrilled to see me again, but he'll just have to deal with it."

Nathan and I retraced our steps to the jail, while several of the witches followed close behind.

"What is it now?" Steve snapped when I entered the reception area.

"Rebecca is missing," I said. "The Head Witch *and* the sceptre have both disappeared."

"Isn't that Madame Grey's responsibility?" he said.

"Madame Grey is searching for her," said Rita from behind me. "I'd suggest you do the same."

"How old is she, eleven?" said Steve. "You'll probably find her hiding in the garden or something. I can send out a search party, but we have two murders to solve and our resources are stretched thin."

"No, they aren't," said Nathan. "I'll fetch my security team and we'll start looking for her right away."

He headed through a door off the reception area, ignoring Steve's grumbling. I, meanwhile, went to join the witches assembled outside the door, talking in loud voices.

"Where is Madame Grey right now?" I asked Rita.

"She's using a tracking spell to make it faster to find her," said Rita. "We haven't a moment to lose."

Alissa hurried up behind me and ran to a breathless halt beside Rita. "Is it true?"

"That Rebecca's missing? Yeah, she is." I indicated the open door of the police station. "Nathan's calling in his team to help look for her, but I can't think where she might have gone."

"Then allow me to help." Samuel appeared behind Alissa and strode up to the police station doors. "If I may offer my assistance, I can move faster than most of the security team."

"Who are you?" Steve demanded.

The vampire entered the police station. "I am Dr Samuel Fairfield."

"You didn't tell me he was a doctor," I muttered to Alissa.

"Seven times over," she whispered back. "He's had a lot of time to kill."

Several decades of it, by the sound of things. I didn't hear Steve's reply, but a moment later, the vampire emerged from the police station again, a satisfied expression on his face.

I gave him a grateful nod. "Thanks so much."

The vampire looked at a point over my shoulder. "I believe it's time to take my leave. This is about to get interesting."

Sure enough, a group of werewolves approached the station, including Chief Donovan. The vampire vanished in an instant, while the chief approached me.

"I heard about your Head Witch," he said. "I will ask the pack to search for her in the forest."

"Really?" I said. "Uh, thank you. Nathan's team is already mobilising, but the more people we can get involved, the better."

Rob caught up to his uncle. "I'll lead a group, too. We'll find her, Blair."

I nodded, encouraged by their show of support. I didn't believe Rebecca had run away, but it was two days until the solstice, and I wouldn't blame her for getting a severe case of nerves despite the progress we'd made in our last training session.

Blythe's accusations came back to me, but there'd be

time enough to question my decisions later. When Rebecca was back home where she belonged.

As though my thoughts had conjured her up, I spotted Blythe herself walking towards the police station. Steeling myself, I walked over to meet her. Her eyes narrowed at the sight of me, and her fists clenched at her sides.

"This is all your fault!" Blythe hissed. "I told you not to encourage her."

Nathan and his team emerged from the police station, and he halted behind me, his gaze on Blythe.

"Go on ahead," I told Nathan. "I'll catch you up once I've dealt with this."

"You've done enough damage," Blythe said.

Nathan shot me a concerned look, but he left Blythe outside the police station and went ahead with the rest of his team.

"Shouldn't you be looking for your sister rather than yelling at me?" I said to Blythe.

"You're the reason she's gone," she spat. "I *told* you not to push her into going ahead with the council's tests. I *knew* something like this would happen."

"I didn't push her into it," I said. "Last I heard, she was prepared and eager to prove herself."

"Exactly!" she said. "You didn't give her the chance to drop out. Now she's either going to be chosen as Head Witch for good, or—"

"Or what?"

"Or someone else will take her place."

I folded my arms. "Who do you think took her?"

"I don't know, Blair. It could have been anyone. She's not at our old house—I checked." Blythe started to sob, her breaths coming too quickly.

"Madame Grey is working on a tracking spell." I took a hesitant step towards her, unsure if she wanted me to comfort her or not. Knowing Blythe, she'd hit me if I tried. "Blythe, panicking won't help any of us. Even if the person who took her stole the sceptre, nobody can claim it until next Samhain, right?"

"No, but it doesn't matter." She sucked in a breath. "Even if we find her, the council will say she's not suited to be Head Witch and remove her from her position, and whoever took her will get exactly what they wanted."

"Not if we find her first." She had a point, though—unfortunately. All they had to do was say that Rebecca had been chosen in error, or that she didn't deserve her position, and the hunters would rally around them. So would the witches who refused to accept a child had been chosen as Head Witch. "Nathan and his security team are looking for her, and so are the werewolves. Even some of the vampires have stepped in. The whole town wants to help you, Blythe, which I would have told you if you hadn't come here screaming accusations."

She blinked in astonishment. Probably, it had never occurred to her that she'd have so much support. After all, she'd probably felt alone for most of her life. No wonder she'd resented me when I'd showed up in town.

"She's right," Alissa said from behind me. "Samuel's taken a group of people to look around the lake. The werewolves are searching the forest. Blythe, if you have any ideas of other people who might have taken her, now's the time to share them."

"Anyone," she said. "For one, the Rosemary witches will have told their entire coven before they were jailed. The nearest town is walkable from here, but with a

166

transportation spell, they might have taken her anywhere."

"Then we'll head up to the border." I struck out in that direction, behind the distant figures of Nathan's security team, with Alissa at my side.

The three Rosemary witches had gone as far as to fake their leader's death so they could claim the sceptre for their own, but Rebecca had thwarted them and unintentionally become the sceptre's new wielder herself. It made sense that their coven would take the first opportunity to steal the sceptre back, but I hadn't seen any strange witches in town, and I'd have thought Madame Grey would be keeping a close watch on the other covens.

"I think you aren't giving your sister enough credit, you know," I added to Blythe. "She's good at magic. Not just with the sceptre, but with her ability, too. You should know that, considering she publicly used her powers on the former Head Witch before she was even chosen as the sceptre's wielder."

"Maybe," she said, "but there are whole covens who'd be happy to use her as a pawn, and I can't even guess which of them might have taken her."

We quickened our pace as we reached the road leading to the university campus, bordered by the forest on the right-hand side. If she was lost in the woods, intentionally or not, finding her would be tricky even with the werewolves on our team. No wonder Madame Grey had opted to use a tracking spell… but would it work if she'd moved too far from the town's boundaries?

Alissa jerked her head towards the path ahead, which merged with the forest on the right-hand side. "I can hear something moving in there."

I tensed, my ears pricked for the sound of Rebecca's voice, but the angry growls of several enraged wolves drowned out all other noise. "You dare accuse me of kidnapping a human?" growled an unfamiliar voice.

"She was sighted near the forest," came Chief Donovan's reply. "And I know all about your ambitions. You think to replace me and put Claude in charge of the pack, don't you? And I suppose you thought the witch would give you an edge. Claude might be ignorant, but I'm not."

"I did not kill anyone, nor did I kidnap a witch," said the other werewolf. More growling and snarling came from the trees as the werewolves squared up to one another. "You're paranoid, Chief, because you know your leadership is under threat from your own nephew."

"Threat?" said the chief. "Do you think I'm unaware of how you've been sneaking around behind my back, making alliances with the other werewolves and sowing distrust?"

"It's how you gained leadership, is it not?" said Claude.

As their growls grew in volume, I backed away from the woods. "I don't think she's in there," I whispered to Alissa.

"Nor me," she said. "Samuel's up there by the border—"

"That's not Samuel," said Blythe. She'd gone very pale. "It's one of them."

I turned towards the border, where Nathan's security team approached a group of people standing on the other side of the campus fence. *Hunters.*

In the woods, the werewolves continued their argument, oblivious to the new arrivals. I hurried uphill away from the forest, Alissa and Blythe on my tail, and caught up to the others at the border.

On the edge of Fairy Falls, Nathan's patrol faced Erin's boyfriend, Buck. Behind him were several men dressed in hiking gear. *He brought other hunters with him?*

"I told you," Buck said. "I have no idea who you're talking about. I thought the Head Witch was part of the Hollyhock Coven, and I wasn't aware there was a new one."

"The new Head Witch, chosen on Samhain, is missing," said one of Nathan's security team. "She was last seen near the forest. Now you show up near our town without good reason and you expect us to believe it's a coincidence?"

"I'm not trespassing," he protested. "And I have no reason to kidnap a witch."

"Be that as it may," said Nathan, "you're also wanted for questioning for your role in two murders which took place close to this very area. Both werewolves were killed by a hunter."

"I did not kill any werewolves." He looked past Nathan, straight at me. "You should know, Blair, why I can't be lying."

Because of my lie-sensing power? His eyes widened a fraction, as though he wanted me to pick up on some hidden meaning, but it was beyond me to tell what it was.

"It wasn't him." Erin stepped up to his side, looking defiantly at her brother. "Believe me."

If it wasn't him or *the werewolves... who did it?* I scanned the other hunters behind Buck, but none of them looked like they might be hiding a frightened eleven-year-old. They also didn't appear to be the same hunters who'd helped Mrs Dailey, either.

"Was she definitely sighted near the woods?" I asked.

"The werewolves say she was, but I think they're a little distracted at the moment."

"I saw a girl going into the woods," said Buck hesitantly. "I didn't know she wasn't supposed to be there."

"She went in there herself?" I said. "Alone?"

My lie-sensing power picked up on no deceit. So either she'd got lost in the woods, or someone had found her wandering and taken her.

A sharp jab in my shoulder made me spin on the spot. Behind me, the pixie fluttered in mid-air, making agitated chittering noises. There was something wrong with one of his wings, which was bent at an awkward angle.

"What're you looking at, Blair?" said Alissa.

Right... the others couldn't see him. "The pixie. I think he might want me to follow him."

I walked with the pixie into the shadow of the nearest thicket of trees. He continued to make agitated noises, circling the trees. A miserable yowl came from the bushes, from someone caught in a tangle of webbing.

Toast. Rebecca's familiar.

"I'm sorry." I clapped a hand to my mouth. "I must have dropped it on my way out of the forest last time. Hang on." I pulled out my wand and cast a couple of cleaning spells until the fluffy ginger cat managed to pull himself free.

"Is she in there?" I whispered to Toast. "She's in trouble?"

He dipped his head.

So my instincts were right. There was someone in the forest who shouldn't be.

I heard a scream from deeper in the woods. *Rebecca.*

"I'm going after her." I took flight with a snap of my

fingers, turning into my fairy form. "Toast—can you fetch Sky? He'll come and help you."

I flew into the trees, following the sound of screaming. The path wound away from the werewolves, deep into tangled trees, until I came to a halt.

The rat shifter, Anton, waited in the clearing, standing clear of a thick web-like net stretched between two trees. Rebecca struggled in mid-air, caught in the net, while the sceptre lay on the ground below.

15

The rat shifter watched Rebecca struggling in the net. "I told you not to scream, girl. You've only made things worse for yourself."

"Why—" I broke off at the sound of rustling in the bushes.

He wasn't alone. Rats lurked throughout the undergrowth, their eyes gleaming, their tails twitching. Small enough to go unnoticed, yet as a collective, they could string up a net to catch a much larger victim. More to the point, they were small enough to sneak around without being seen by anyone not close to their size. They were perfectly capable of slipping into a hunters' camp and stealing their property.

They could even gnaw away at a tree until it fell on an unsuspecting werewolf—or sneak into a coffee shop and slip a potion into a drink without being seen by the human staff.

"You did it," I said. "You stole the nets—and the gun, too. *You're* the one who killed the werewolves."

The rat shifter tilted his head at me. "I really hoped you wouldn't come here, Blair. You should have left me alone."

"I wouldn't have suspected you if you hadn't kidnapped the Head Witch," I said.

"I didn't kidnap her. She wandered into my territory of her own accord."

"A likely story," I said heatedly. "Why kill Alec or Julius? The werewolves haven't done anything to you."

"Haven't done anything?" A chorus of shrieks from the other rats punctuated his words. "They've encroached on our territory until there's almost nothing left of it. We were promised this part of the forest when we first moved in, but the pack chief conveniently forgot, and instead continued to expand his own territory until we had almost nothing left."

My hands clenched. "That's no excuse to commit murder. One of the people you killed was just a kid."

His rat-like nose twitched. "Have you any idea how many of *my* people the werewolves have trodden into the dirt? We mean nothing to them, at all. They're far more concerned with their petty squabbles than the rest of us."

"You wanted the pack to be distracted so you could steal their territory, didn't you?" I said to Anton. "They're running around looking for Rebecca while you held her captive here. Don't pretend you didn't plan on taking advantage."

"Because the werewolves have dominated the forest for long enough," he said. "Besides, the chief and his nephew have been at one another's throats ever since Claude got old enough to present a challenge. I hardly care who wins, but their conflict will bring a long-overdue end to the werewolves' dominance."

"You have no idea what you've done, do you?" I glanced at Rebecca. "She's Head Witch. The local coven inspectors are coming to town any day now, and if they find out you did this, there'll be hell to pay. Not to mention you got a lot of innocent people into trouble."

"Did you know these traps were originally intended to be used on small shifters like us?" he said, as though I hadn't spoken. "They were never banned by the covens. The hunters only stopped using them because they proved inconvenient to their own people, but the witches were happy to let them continue to get away with it."

"Look, take your grievances to Madame Grey if you have to. Just leave Rebecca out of it."

It was hopeless trying to get through to him. He didn't *care* about the covens, only about his revenge. And he didn't care if Rebecca suffered as a consequence.

"Nobody in this town ever thinks of those smaller than themselves," he went on. "No, not even the witches do. They backed up the chief's promise and then betrayed us."

My fingers inched towards my wand. I wasn't lost on what a swarm of rats could do to a person—I'd witnessed a group of mice single-handedly take down the town's former wand-maker, after all, and didn't particularly want to experience the same myself. But if I didn't get Rebecca out of that web, we were both screwed.

"You know, normally I'd tell you to pick on someone your own size, but…" I whipped out my wand and waved it at the net. The sceptre slid closer to the net, but before

Rebecca could free herself, a branch snapped from the tree above my head, hurtling towards me.

I flew out of reach, and the branch crashed down into the undergrowth. Beating my wings, I turned to Rebecca, but sticky strands clung to my face and hands. The rat shifters laughed.

Oh, no.

Another rat shifter climbed up the branch alongside me and kicked my wand out of my hand while I struggled to free myself from the web.

"There," said Anton, facing me with a satisfied expression on his face. "Maybe the covens will take us seriously now we have two of their best witches."

"You're going to use us as hostages?" I squirmed in the net. "Look, the solstice is in two days, and if the local council's inspectors come to town and find us gone—"

"They will be forced to take us seriously," he finished.

The other rats chittered in agreement. They were caught up in the thrill of having power over us and had no idea of the damage Rebecca's absence would do, let alone the sceptre. A fine mess I'd made of this rescue mission.

"Sorry," she whispered. "I got nervous before the ceremony and went to practise near the forest. Next thing I know, I'm stuck in a net."

"Would you believe this is the second time it's happened to me?" I struggled and flailed, but my hands remained ensnared in the sticky web. *I have to get us both out.* Without my wand, or my fairy magic. All I could think of to do was call…

Rebecca muttered something under her breath. Then the branches parted, rustling, and two heads popped out.

"MIAOW," said Sky.

"Miaow," said Toast, in proud tones.

"Thanks, Toast," I said. "Now… you know how cats feel about rats, don't you?"

Anton looked at the newcomers in horror, while his fellow rats backed away into the undergrowth. They might be able to bring down a full-grown werewolf or human, but the sight of two felines was another thing entirely.

"I don't suppose your claws can cut the webs?" I called to the cats.

"Miaow." Sky didn't move.

Then a voice drifted through the trees. "Who is there?"

Wait—I knew that voice. Bramble the elf. Toast hadn't just fetched Sky, but he'd brought the elves here, too. Most likely they were the first people he'd managed to find, with the werewolves being too busy fighting one another to get involved in the search.

"Over here!" I shouted. "It's Blair and Rebecca. We got caught in a trap, and we need help."

Bramble and Twig emerged from the bushes a moment later, staring at the webs in confusion. "What is this?"

"The rat shifters," I said. "They trapped us in here. Rebecca is the Head Witch, and it's the solstice in two days, so I'd really appreciate it if you gave us a hand getting out of this net."

Rebecca gaped at the newcomers. "You're real? I've never seen an elf before."

"We are." Bramble snapped his fingers and the branches moved downward. My feet touched the ground, as did Rebecca's, but despite my best efforts, my hands and arms remained ensnared.

Then a flash of purple light drew my eyes to the undergrowth. Toast poked his head out of a bush, holding the sceptre in his mouth so Rebecca could reach it. As she touched it, the web broke, allowing her to take the sceptre from him. Face furrowed in concentration, she tightened her grip and waved it in a circle. At once, the web released us, and I landed on my feet with relief. Sky padded over to me, holding my wand in his mouth.

I stroked Sky behind the ears. "You just wanted me to think you'd chosen to leave me hanging up there, didn't you?"

"Miaow," he said.

I looked around for the rat shifters and spotted several pairs of beady eyes lurking in the bushes.

"Let's draw them out," I told Rebecca. "Ready?"

"Ready."

I waved my wand, and Rebecca lifted the sceptre. The tattered remains of the net flew over the bushes and landed on top of the fleeing rat shifters. Several escaped, but the elves blocked the paths, forcing them back into the net.

Within a few short minutes, the rats were trussed up in a coating of sticky webbing. The elves disappeared into the woods, but our familiars supervised with twitching tails until every rat was captured.

"We'll have to levitate it out of the forest," I said.

Rebecca lifted the sceptre. "No problem."

The rats squealed. Some of them tried shifting to human form and back to rats again, but no matter how many times they tried, they couldn't break free of the web. Once we had them in the air, we hurried along the forest path with our captives in tow, back towards the entrance.

Beside the border, the security team remained in a standoff with Erin and Buck.

"I'm here!" Rebecca said. "Not kidnapped. It was the rat shifters."

Blythe ran over at once, halting before her with a gasp. "You're safe!"

I flicked my wand and deposited the rat shifters' tangled web outside the forest. "Where's Chief Donovan? We found the people who killed the two werewolves."

"Chief Donovan is dealing with a situation," said Rita.

Meaning, he and his fellow werewolves were still tearing into one another. After my narrow escape, I'd rather not step into the middle of that one.

"Rats?" said one of the hunters. "Rat shifters killed werewolves? Don't be ridiculous."

"It's true." I walked towards the group at the border. "Anton is their leader, but I can't tell which rat he is."

"There's a simple way." Rita pushed out of the crowd and waved her wand at the net. At once, it expanded, and the rats shifted into human form, landing in an uncomfortable-looking heap. Anton groaned, spitting out obscenities.

"The others went along with his plan," I added. "He wanted the werewolves to sit up and take notice of his pack, and he didn't care who got hurt in the process. He stole the gun from Buck, along with this net, and intended to take over the pack's territory while they were distracted."

Everyone broke into conversation, accusations flying left and right. While the hunters and witches shouted at one another, Blythe comforted her sister, while Alissa made her way over to me.

"Where's Madame Grey?" I asked her in an undertone.

"Still searching the forest with the police," she whispered back. "I've no doubt she'll find any stragglers, if there are any."

"We have to tell her we found Rebecca." I shot a concerned look at Buck and the other hunters. "Before word gets back to the inspectors."

"You found her?" The trees parted, and Claude limped out of the forest, completely naked. Behind him were several other werewolves, all equally unclothed, including the Chief. While they all looked a little battered, at least nobody else had been killed.

"There it is," Claude growled. "I told the chief it was nonsense for him to accuse me of kidnapping the girl."

"You're the one who told me to go deeper into the woods," Rebecca said.

"Really?" said Chief Donovan. "Interesting how she ended up lost in a part of the woods humans shouldn't be able to get to, isn't it?"

Rebecca shrank away from the chief. "I'm sorry. I assumed the chief's nephew wouldn't send me in the wrong direction."

Chief Donovan turned on his nephew. "What did you hope to gain from getting the Head Witch lost in the woods, exactly?"

Claude's mouth opened and closed. "It was just a joke. I knew she was a friend of Blair's…"

"And you hoped the pack would assume I was responsible?" The chief's eyes narrowed at the net of captive rats.

"I am still the pack leader, and you aren't fit to challenge me."

It would have been a tenser conversation to witness if most of the people involved had been wearing a stitch of clothing.

"Nathan," said one of the hunters at the border. With a start, I recognised him as Jay, Nathan and Erin's older brother. *Oh, no.* "Please explain the meaning of this."

Nathan spoke up. "It seems this pack of rat shifters decided to steal the hunters' property in an attempt to sow discord within the werewolf pack. There will be no punishment except for the guilty."

"Then whose gun did they steal?" said Jay. "Yours?"

Buck stepped forwards. "Mine."

"He didn't use the gun," Erin put in. "He came here to meet me, not to hurt anyone."

"She's right," said Buck. "I was staying in the next town over while Erin looked for a job."

"You're still employed by the hunters," said Jay. "Would you give up your duty so easily?"

He gave Jay a defiant look. "To keep my fiancée safe? Yes, I will."

Nathan and his older brother both stared openly at Erin.

"You *what?*" Jay thundered. "You're engaged to—him?"

"Yes, I am," said Erin. "Got a problem with that?"

Everyone seemed to have forgotten all about the werewolves. Claude and his fellow wolves sloped back into the forest with their tails between their legs—metaphorically, since they were still in the form of naked humans. Chief Donovan, Rob and his fellow werewolves, meanwhile, surrounded the squirming net full of captured rat shifters.

Finally, Madame Grey emerged from the woods, startling everyone into silence. "My tracking spell led me in circles," she said. "Who is the culprit, pray tell? I assume you're all here arguing with one another because you found the person responsible."

"Them." I indicated the net filled with rat shifters. "You might need to disentangle them before their trial."

Rita moved to her side. "These shifters are responsible for the deaths of two people. Take them in, and as for you —" She addressed Jay—"I'd kindly ask you hunters to deal with your issues in your own time."

As the group began to break apart, Blythe moved closer to me. "Blair. They're here... they're right here."

"Who?" I frowned at the hunters. "What do you mean?"

"Look at Buck. What is he?"

I did so. For the first time, I *really* looked at him—and my paranormal-sensing power hit a wall. Like it had only once before.

My heartbeat kicked into gear, but I forced myself to keep looking, until gradually, the glamour peeled away, revealing pointed ears. Wings. Shining skin. Glitter.

Buck was a fairy.

Erin knew. There was no way she didn't. Looking at Buck, I couldn't believe I hadn't realised he was glamoured. He'd seemed vaguely familiar to me when I'd first set eyes on him, but he was the one who must have seen through my glamour right off. Even if he hadn't, Erin might have told him I was half-fairy. So that's why he was confident I'd know he was telling the truth. He hadn't lied —*couldn't* lie, if the rumours about fairies were true.

Blythe leaned in to speak to me again. "He's not the

only one," she whispered. "The only fairy, I mean. There are others."

"What—in town? How?"

"Not in town."

In a horrible jolt, I remembered my paranormal-sensing power's reaction to seeing the leader of the hunters. Inquisitor Hare. How I'd picked him out as a paranormal, yet I hadn't been able to figure out what type. Because my powers didn't work on other people like me.

Inquisitor Hare is a fairy. The person responsible for jailing my dad had been one of the fairies all along.

16

The representatives of the local witch council showed up promptly on the morning of the solstice, filing into our office. Their leader, Angelica, was a tall woman with neatly curled black hair who wore a pressed suit that looked like it'd been ironed while she was wearing it. She and Veronica eyed one another with open dislike as she walked into the reception area to Callie's cheery smile. So this was the woman who had the authority to declare whether Dritch & Co would be allowed to continue operating or whether we'd be closing our doors for good.

Rob pounced on her the instant she entered our office, insisting on handing her a mug of coffee, and put on his best customer-facing voice. Angela's sharp eyes darted around the room as though looking for a speck of dust that was out of place. "A paranormal recruitment office, Veronica? You're still trying to make something of your absurd ideas? Gladys always said you could have been in her place if you applied yourself, but... here we are."

"I think you'll find, Angela, that I have been successfully running this business for a number of years." Veronica fixed on a false smile. "I started this company to fill a gap in the market. So many paranormals haven't the time to seek out suitable employees, so we use our considerable resources to track down the best candidate for the job."

"Very extensive resources," Bethan put in. "I'm Veronica's daughter and assistant."

"Oh, you're the child she had with the shifter," said Angela, wrinkling her nose. "I believe that's the moment Gladys gave up on her in despair. She could have been in my place, you know, if she hadn't been attached to her wild flights of fancy."

She's a real piece of work. I understood why Veronica disliked her so much, but Rob wore his usual smile and indicated the stack of papers on Bethan's desk. "There's a high demand for our services, as you can see. We see it as our duty to help out everyone who needs us."

"Even the leader of the local werewolf pack has used our services," I added. "Several times."

Angela didn't look convinced. "Why would the werewolves possibly need a group of witches to help them search for a job?"

"Have you ever seen a werewolf who's never been outside of the forest walk into a job fair?" I said. "They don't even know when it's acceptable to wear clothes or not. Trust me, it's better for us to handle those cases before unleashing them on the job market."

"Not all of us are house-trained," added Rob. "Also, before I started working here, they exposed a wand-maker who faked his own death."

"That was mostly Blair," Bethan put in. "She also helped save his missing apprentices. If he hadn't hired Dritch & Co, we never would have known they were cursed to spend the rest of their lives as rodents."

Angela and her fellow inspectors turned to me. "You're the one who trained the Head Witch, yes?"

"I am," I confirmed. "She'll be showing you her skills later this afternoon."

"Interesting," said Angela. "Why did you choose to work at Dritch & Co?"

"Because they helped me figure out who I am." That, I realised as I spoke the words, was the absolute truth.

"I've heard a number of disturbing stories of employees quitting, bodies found in the office, ghosts…"

"Oh, yes, we exorcised a ghost from this very office," said Bethan, undeterred. "As for the bodies, someone saw fit to pin a murder accusation on our boss, but we solved the case. Or Blair solved it, anyway."

My face flushed. "Not just me. I had help. Not every employee who's tried to work here has been the right fit, but we have a great team together and Veronica is absolutely the right person to run this office."

It was Veronica's turn to blush. "Oh, Angela, the printer wants to talk to you."

The printer broke into a loud rendition of *Thank you for the Music* and spat a handful of papers out. Lizzie picked them up, handing them to a stupefied Angela.

Veronica leaned in. "There's a summary of recent events which sets the record straight. Would you like to come and see the inside of my office? I have a space theme this week."

"No… That all seems to be in order." She inched towards the door. "And thank you for the coffee."

"You can thank Lizzie for that," said Veronica.

Lizzie emerged from behind her computer. "Don't forget to take one of our business cards."

She handed Angela a stack of business cards—another creation of the printer and Lizzie's last-minute graphic design skills—and Angela backed out of the office with visible relief.

As the door closed, Veronica mimed dusting off her hands. "That's that taken care of. Admirable, all of you."

"We just did what we normally do," said Callie, from the reception area.

"Because nobody else wants to deal with it," I said.

"That's our selling point," said Bethan. "Let's face it, there would be a lot *more* chaos without us around."

"Some credit goes to our amazing coffee machine." Lizzie retreated to her desk. "I asked it to put a mood-booster in her coffee. Nothing illegal, don't worry. It's not like it was a lucky latte."

I had to admit, I wished I'd sneaked some of it myself. Rebecca's assessment would be later this afternoon while I was still at work, and I wouldn't be allowed to watch. I'd just have to hope Rebecca remembered everything we'd practised together.

Over the last two days, the town had more or less returned to normal—or what passed for normal in Fairy Falls, at any rate. The rat shifters who'd been involved in Anton's coup were facing a long stint behind bars—after the pack chief had doled out his own punishment, that is. The pack's rebellion had been quelled, the hunters had left town, and I'd survived to see the solstice.

Too bad I wouldn't be getting to see my dad after all.

Nothing fairy-related had appeared today, unless you counted my cat getting into a fight with a local stray. Even Erin hadn't got back in touch, so I'd have to wait to talk to her about her boyfriend. I mean, fiancé.

Buck was a fairy. A *fairy*, like me. More to the point, so was the Inquisitor. He must be wearing one serious glamour to fool everyone into thinking he was human, unless he'd ordered his fellow hunters to keep his identity a secret. Like Nathan's father—not that I'd mentioned it to Nathan yet either. He and the security team had been run off their feet the last two days, and I'd decided to wait until Rebecca's test was over before dropping any more bombshells.

I shouldn't have reason to worry. The Inquisitor didn't know I knew his secret, and he, at least, wasn't a mind-reader. But it explained why he'd tried to recruit me, and why he'd spoken to me as though we were in on a shared joke. What it *didn't* explain was why he'd arrested my dad.

I'd written dozens of letters to my dad in the last week, yet I'd seen neither hide nor hair of the pixie since he'd appeared outside the forest two days ago.

Is the Inquisitor a fairy? Is that why you wanted me to leave town?

Was he responsible for my mum's death?

I'd met a ghost in the local cemetery who'd hinted that the *fairies* had caused her death. At the time, I'd seen no possible link with the hunters, but now my dad's concern about our correspondence being intercepted made a lot more sense. After all, the pixie's glamour wasn't as effective around other fairies, and for all I knew, the Inquisitor or one of the others had already cut off our line of communication. I was taking a major risk in trying to contact my dad at all, but what else could I do?

When work finished for the day, I went into the reception area to talk to Callie.

"Is the chief okay?" I asked her. "And the rest of the pack?"

She nodded. "Yeah. He let Claude stay, but he has people keeping an eye on him in case he tries to raise another rebellion. So far, he hasn't tried anything. Making a fool of himself in front of the hunters hurt his ego, I think."

"He'll have a long hard think before he tries to displace his uncle again," added Rob. "How's your witch friend?"

"Rebecca? Her testing should be over soon." I checked the time. "I'd better go and meet her."

I walked to the witches' headquarters, my nerves beginning to spike. As I reached the building, the council's representatives walked out, but I couldn't tell from their expressions whether it was good news or bad news.

Heart thumping, I pushed open the door and walked over to Madame Grey's office.

Rebecca emerged a moment later. "I passed!" she said, her voice somewhat squeaky.

"Of course you did," said Madame Grey from behind her. "The sceptre picks the bearer based on many qualities, and you possess them all, judging by your actions on Samhain."

Rebecca's cheeks turned pink. "Uh, so when will I be going to visit the other towns?"

"In the new year," said Madame Grey. "I'll be with you the whole time. We managed to negotiate an agreement where you'll get to finish your education before taking on any major duties."

"I'm really glad it went well," I said. "It sounds like the town passed the inspection, too."

"We did." Madame Grey gave me a rare smile. "Good job, Blair."

I couldn't quite meet her eyes. I hadn't told Madame Grey about my new discovery about the Inquisitor's identity, and while this was the first time I'd seen her in two days, I didn't want to dampen Rebecca's success by bringing up the subject.

"We'll discuss your first visit after the holidays," said Madame Grey. "In the meantime, take a break, both of you—you've earned it."

While Rebecca bounded off to meet her guardian and tell her the good news, I found Alissa waiting outside the building.

"I take it the exam went well?" she said.

"Rebecca did great," I said. "I thought you were at work."

"My shift finished early," she said. "I told Samuel to look in the library for what you asked for, but you know, you could have just asked him in person."

"I didn't want to have to explain my entire history." I glanced around to make sure nobody was listening in. I hadn't told Alissa about the Inquisitor, either, but given Samuel's mind-reading talents, word might spread through half the town even if she didn't tell a soul. Still, that hadn't stopped me from requesting every book in the library on fairies in the hope that I might find an explanation about how one of them had come to be in charge of the region's paranormal hunters. My hopes weren't high, but it was better than nothing.

"There isn't much information, but he did find this." Alissa held up the smallest example of a textbook I'd ever seen. It looked more like a pamphlet.

I took it from her and read, "How to negotiate with one of the fairies: Don't. That's all?"

"He did say it was a little brief," she said in apologetic tones. "There really isn't much in the way of information on fairies in the library."

"Don't worry about it," I said. "You and Samuel are good, then? I can't believe he's a doctor. Several times over."

"Yeah… we are." She smiled. "Don't worry, he hasn't turned me into a vampire."

"Glad you haven't completely lost your senses."

"Oi," she said. "What about you and Nathan?"

"I'm meant to be meeting him at the pub now. He said he has a surprise for me."

Her brows shot up. "What kind of surprise?"

"No idea, but I'm looking forward to finding out."

At least I was reasonably confident on it having nothing to do with the fairies. Or the hunters. Erin was still out of town, though her boyfriend—or rather, fiancé —hadn't been charged for accidentally letting his gun fall into the wrong hands. The worst that could happen was that he might be pressed into leaving the hunters, but it sounded like he had every intention of doing so, and soon.

Did *he* know about the Inquisitor? Maybe. I didn't think he knew Inquisitor Hare had tried to recruit me, because I hadn't told Erin.

I did my best to forget the Inquisitor as I approached the Troll's Tavern, where Nathan was already waiting inside. As I pushed the door open, Sky padded up to me and shoved a note into my shoe. Then he walked away from the pub, leaving me to enter alone.

I found Nathan sitting at our usual table. "What's up, Blair?"

"Sky just gave me this." I pulled the note out of my shoe but didn't open it. "Are there any vampires in here?"

"Vampires? No. Why?"

"Just wanted to be sure nobody's listening to my thoughts."

I unfolded the note. It said, *I'm sorry I couldn't see you, Blair.*

A few lines followed that I couldn't read. They weren't written in English, or even using the letters I knew.

I held up the note to show Nathan, and he frowned. "I can't read that, Blair. Is it written in the fairy language?"

"No idea." Surely not. After all, if it was, then the Inquisitor would be able to read it. I slipped the note into my pocket and ordered a drink by tapping the menu. "I guess the pixie's taking a holiday if he's sending my cat to deliver notes."

No wonder he'd been avoiding me lately. He was probably scared for his own safety, considering the leader of the hunters could see through glamour. I hadn't realised he'd taken such a major risk in carrying notes in and out of the prison.

"I thought you could block mind-readers," Nathan said.

"*You* can't." I looked down at the table, my pulse racing.

"And I want to tell you something important, but I don't want either of us to get into trouble for it."

"Relax, Blair." He rested his hand over mine. "What did you want to tell me?"

"The hunters have fairies working for them," I whispered. "I guess you knew that, since Erin is dating one of them."

"I didn't know until you did, Blair."

"I really hope *Erin* did."

Nathan lifted his hand from mine, his gaze fixing on something behind my shoulder. "Erin, what are you doing here?"

I twisted in my seat as Erin grabbed a chair from a nearby table and pulled it up to join us.

"Erin." Had she been listening to our conversation? "You know we're on a date, right?"

"I wanted to talk to you before I go home. Not permanently," she added. "I'm going to visit my family for the holidays. Anyway—I just wanted to say that I knew. What Buck is, I mean. I wanted to tell you, but I wasn't sure if you already knew."

"Is it common for fairies to work for the hunters?" I asked. "Because I thought the hunters were mostly non-paranormals."

"Mostly, but there are a few exceptions," said Erin. "He's half human, half fairy. He told me on our first date, so I wouldn't freak out."

No wonder she'd been unfazed when I'd been revealed as a fairy in front of her family. What in the world did her dad think, though? Well, since Buck was a hunter as well as a fairy, he'd probably find him less objectionable than he did me, but still.

Nathan's father... *he* was human. I was fairly certain on that point. But that didn't mean he knew nothing about the paranormals secretly working for the hunters. He *had* known that Tanith Wildflower had somehow made an enemy of the fairies, and that was why she'd died. Erin had already said she knew nothing about that, and yet...

"Do you know any other fairies working for them?" I asked.

"The hunters? No. Like I said, it's rare. And Buck was pretty nervous about telling me."

True. The knot in my chest loosened. I felt a lot better about Erin's decision to move to Fairy Falls now the hunters had been revealed to have had nothing to do with the werewolves' deaths. As a bonus, I wouldn't be the only fairy in town for once, either. "Thanks for letting me know."

"Anyway, I have to run." She got to her feet. "See you around, Blair."

Nathan frowned over my shoulder at her. "I hope she knows what she's doing. I didn't know Buck was a fairy, but I got the impression he would prefer that information not to spread among the hunters."

"The Inquisitor is one of them." I dropped my voice. "He's one of the fairies."

Nathan shook his head. "No..."

"It's true," I said. "Blythe told me. He was glamoured, and that's why he confused me when I first saw him. My paranormal-sensing power doesn't work on other fairies."

His eyes widened. "The Inquisitor... I've only seen him a handful of times, but he's been to my house. I would have known..."

"He's good at using glamour. Really good." I sucked in a breath. "When he tried to recruit me, I was sure he knew something I didn't. I always thought it was weird that he wanted to hire me, considering my parents. Now I know why."

I did... and I didn't. Even if their leader was a fairy, why had I caught his attention? Because of my dad? Or because of the fairies who'd caused my mum's death? Questions buzzed in my mind, filling me with restless energy.

Nathan's calm gaze kept me grounded. "I didn't know, Blair. I always assumed my colleagues were human."

Then was there a big cover-up, surely. Unless the fairies preferred to keep to themselves, but why would they choose to join the hunters over living in a paranormal community like Fairy Falls?

It hadn't always been like this. Fairies had lived here once. In fact, they'd founded the town to begin with. So what had changed?

Buck and I were going to have a good long chat when we next met face to face, that was for sure.

"The fairies are linked to the hunters," I said, "and it's all tied to what happened to my family. Do you think your dad knows?"

"I don't see why he would," he said. "I also had no idea the Inquisitor might be paranormal at all. Granted, his background was always a mystery, but I assumed he had personal reasons for leading the local hunters' branch."

Was *that* what the elves had meant when they'd said the fairies were coming back? They had no love for the hunters, after all. Blythe, knew, and I bet her mother did as well. At least *she* was behind bars. It went a long way to explaining Blythe's instant dislike of me when I'd moved to town—not because she thought I was a criminal, but because she thought my presence would draw the hunters to town. And she'd been dead right.

I pulled my drink closer to me. "Enough about my messed-up family life. What is it you wanted to talk to me about?"

Nathan said, "I've asked for some time off. I think we should get out of town for a while. Just for the new year."

"You mean an actual holiday?" I said. "Not a date that gets interrupted by murders, or gargoyles, or fairies. I know excitement seems to follow us everywhere, but it'll be nice to take a step back for once."

"I hoped you'd say that." He took my hand across the table. "I have a few ideas, but do you have any particular requirements? I can find a nice seaside town so we can spend the new year on the beach."

I raised an eyebrow. "With England's weather, that might be hoping for too much. Perhaps there's a secret witch community in Spain, but that's a little outside my budget. Also, my foster parents might be coming back for a visit after the holidays and I don't want to miss them. Or Rebecca's first event as Head Witch, whenever that is. But yes. I'd love to."

He nodded. "Do you want to stay here for Christmas and go away for the new year?"

"That would be perfect."

"Good." He smiled. "Any preferences, then?"

I cast my mind around. "Is there anywhere with a really good library?"

"Library? Why?"

I held up the note from my dad. "I think I'm supposed to work out what this means. I already searched the library on campus, and there's nothing there. But if you'd rather hang out on the beach, I'm good with that."

"We can do both," said Nathan. "I know just the place."

ABOUT THE AUTHOR

Elle Adams lives in the middle of England, where she spends most of her time reading an ever-growing mountain of books, planning her next adventure, or writing. Elle's books are humorous mysteries with a paranormal twist, packed with magical mayhem.

She also writes urban and contemporary fantasy novels as Emma L. Adams.

Find Elle on Facebook at https://www.facebook.com/pg/ElleAdamsAuthor/

Made in the USA
Las Vegas, NV
22 September 2024

95647261R00121